UP AND OUT

ZEPHYR BOOKS

Classic short works

1. GAUTIER One of Cleopatra's Nights
2. GRAND The Yellow Leaf
3. POWYS The Owl, the Duck, and — Miss Rowe! Miss Rowe!
4. BERRIDGE The Story of Stanley Brent
5. ERTEL A Greedy Peasant
6. RICHARDSON The End of a Childhood
7. POWYS Up and Out

UP AND OUT

A MYSTERY-TALE

by

JOHN COWPER POWYS

Zephyr Books

SANDNESS
MICHAEL WALMER
2020

Up and Out first published 1957 with another novella

This edition published 2020

by

Michael Walmer
North House
Melby
Sandness
Shetland ZE2 9PL

ISBN 978-0-6489204-3-4 hardcover

To

L. U. WILKINSON

Up and Out

Gor Goginog is my name and I am writing this in the English language for a special and peculiar reason.

I was an orphan in an orphanage and I was never told who my parents were. I was born in a Welsh quarrytown called Blaenau-Ffestiniog under conditions that made me not only speak in two languages when I first learnt to speak but also made me think in two languages when I first learnt to think. I became indeed at a very early age, in fact either at five or at six, seized with a desperate mania for words: yes! for words as in their essential nature they really are, that is to say the expression of every kind of thought, emotion, feeling, sensation and idea that can possibly enter from outside, or can possibly spring up from inside, any imaginable or conceivable living creature. In a childish way, but whether in accordance with my appearance as a small boy I cannot say, I was endowed with an intelligence a great deal beyond my years, and with a shrewdness in coaxing, cajoling, and seducing to my purpose, whatever purpose at that particular moment it might be, not only older boys and older girls but grown-up people of both sexes.

In response to my fervent solicitations a middle-aged American couple who visited Blaenau took me with them as their adopted son, for they themselves were childless, to New York City, and here I remained until Rhitha, a girl I had courted when a boy and who lived at Llandderfel, came to New York. And do you know what, apart from courting Rhitha, I spent my boyhood and young manhood upon? Upon one sole thing; upon inventing a universal Western Language! It sounds crazy, and of course some of you will accuse me of playing the copycat to that invented language called Esperanto and even to the inspired author of "Finnegan's Wake." But any way my purpose was to mingle and mix up in one verbal paint-pot, or let us say upon one syllabic palette, all the most characteristically national and all the most local and idiomatic expressions in English, French, Italian, Spanish, Dutch, Portuguese, Swedish, and Laplandish, and out of these multi-national composite sounds to create a lexiconic instrument through which the whole body, soul, and spirit of the men, women, and children of Europe could be expressed.

I was well advanced in my teens when I first courted Rhitha. In fact we were both seventeen—only as my birthday was the last day of November in the old year, and hers was the last day of April in the new year she was a few months the younger. Rhitha, like myself, was Welsh. She came from a small village not very far from Blaenau called Llandderfel, and she had for the patron-saint, patron-god or patron-devil of her village a deep, blind, unshakable awe and reverence which included the saint-devil's war-horse.

I was a tall lad and Rhitha was tall and slender. She had long white arms and beautiful legs and I had long strong arms and very athletic legs. Like Rhitha I had a small waist and deft, rapid, nimble movements. Indeed I would say that it was the peculiarly quick reciprocity between my body and my mind that was at the heart of all I felt and of all I did. Everything I saw, heard, touched, tasted and smelt, was embraced, like the body of my loved one, by an exquisite concordance of my whole nature. And the curious thing is that Rhitha and I, allowing for her being a girl and my being a boy, were almost identical in these respects. She, too, was astonishingly rapid in all her movements. She, too, quite obviously to all who watched her, was wont to throw her entire being, "body, soul and spirit," as the conventional phrase puts it, into every single thing she took in, whether it were a curve in a statue, a colour in a picture, a scent in a leaf, or a series of notes in a tune. Over the most evasive things in nature, a dragon-fly's eye, a lizard's foot, a minnow's tail, the slimy gloss on the spine of a black slug, the far-away wide-curving horizon of the ocean, Rhitha would hover with the same devouring enchantment as I felt for such things.

And we were the same too in our moral emotions. The one evil which neither of us could endure was cold-blooded cruelty; and when in our prowlings about New York City—which, in some respects, without being conceited, for you can easily be a very cowardly crusader, I might call crusades against cruelty and which were much more exciting to both of us than any film or television or opera or play could be—we chanced at last to come upon what the vivisectors were doing to dogs, cats, monkeys, and all sorts of other animals, we soon realized that we had found the worst example of unspeakable wickedness to be discovered in the whole of our modern world. We are both equally clever at getting round people and influencing people and moulding people to our immediate purpose; so working together, Rhitha with all a woman's wiles, and I with the guile of a Borgia or the statecraft of a Lord Burleigh, we soon got an entrance into all the cruellest and wickedest vivisection laboratories in New York City.

To say we were horrified and shocked at what we saw is as people say now "to put it mildly." Nor were our feelings mollified by learning that the tolerant and indulgent neutral government of India was sending this very year over two thousand monkeys in order that there should not be a month's or even a week's relaxation of the excruciating pain inflicted by the descendants of Cro-Magnon cave-men, many of them with more than a dash of Neanderthal-blood in their veins upon their innocent ancestors who had not yet had the cunning to come down from the trees.

We were far from blaming the medical profession for what we saw of these infernal cruelties. We soon discovered that ordinary doctors know absolutely nothing of these horrors. What struck us as most appalling were certain attempts we found going on to graft living animals upon one another. We found for instance a certain group of vivisectors intensely pleased with themselves for having produced by vivisection a dog with two heads. We got a glimpse of this phenomenon; and we found it hard to forget the pathetic way in which these two heads, who evidently felt themselves to be, and had every reason for such a feeling, two separate identities, with separate minds and bodies, watched each other and licked each other and evidently said to each other: "We have heard about the tortures inflicted by the Holy Office of the

Inquisition but even the Holy Office didn't graft a Wesleyan baby on the neck of a Baptist baby."

Never had vivisectors brought forward all their favourite humbug about the life of one precious human child being well worth the excruciating sufferings of a million dogs, and a million cats, not to mention two or three million monkeys, with so little effect as in the case of Rhitha and me. We made our way hurriedly to Patchin Place, just off Sixth Avenue, in which there grew a gigantic ailanthus tree that we had come, ever since we first met, to regard as our "Sacred Grove" of refuge, though it was a lonely and a rather forlorn tree and also an extremely proud and very unbending tree.

Here then we got into the habit of standing, perhaps recalling the days when our monkey-ancestors came down from such a tree, but at any rate in a mood of savage anger at the cruelty of these vivisectors, each of us with a hand against the trunk of the tree. It was on a certain Wednesday we were standing here, the day of the week dedicated by the Anglo-Saxons to Woden and by the Romans and the Welsh to Mercury. The lights of the city were lit, and every now and then a tram or a taxi could be heard. But there were only small floating clouds of very thin mist and vapour between our ailanthus tree and the "enormous and delicate" sky.

The evening was well advanced by this time and the sky was growing black. But its blackness was the reverse of a thick, dense, opaque, heavy darkness. For once it happened, as I told myself afterwards, and when we recalled what we experienced Rhitha entirely agreed with me, that the sky looked what it actually was—a portion of the vast unending limitless gulf in which the galaxies and the nebulae and the stars of our system and the stars of all the other systems live and die even as we do ourselves.

"Listen my heart," I said. "Let us pray to the King of the Gods by his three-fold name. Let us pray to him by his name Jehovah, as the simpler among the Jews called him, though every Rabbi would explain to them that in reality he was *nameless*. Let us pray to him by his name Jupiter or Jove, as the Romans worshipped him. And let us pray to him by his name Zeus the Son of Kronos as the Greeks worshipped him."

Never afterwards did I, Gor Goginog of Blaenau, forget Rhitha's profile as I saw it outlined at that moment between the lighted window of a small ground-floor apartment and the sacred tree of our Grove of Worship.

"What shall we pray to the King of the Gods to do?" Rhitha asked.

I pressed the knuckles of the hand that held hers against the bark of the ailanthus tree, pressed them so hard that it hurt. And I thought to myself, "I'm glad it hurt. When people make vows to the immortals it's a good thing to arrange, as the old Athenians used to do, for some kind of offering. My offering now is this pain in my knuckles."

"I'll tell you exactly, my heart, what we'll pray for tonight. We'll pray to Jehovah-Jove-Zeus that every single creature being vivisected tomorrow shall feel no pain. It's the day the Saxons have dedicated to their war-god Thor, and the day we Welsh call Dydd Iau, the day of Jove. But never mind what we call it. As Goethe says, 'The Name is sound and smoke obscuring Heaven's clear glow!' Yes, let us pray to Jove, O my treasure, 'in good set terms.' Let us pray that every single animal, dog, cat, monkey or any other, they will be torturing tomorrow in this city shall become, until it dies, wholly and totally devoid of the capacity to feel anything at all! *That* will worry these devils! We couldn't possibly worry them more than by immunising and petrifying and atrophying and de-sensitizing every victim in their laboratories! Have you prayed as I told you, Rhitha?"

Rhitha, who had been pressing her forehead against the trunk of the ailanthus, moved her neck a little so that she could give a slight nod in reply to this question.

"But you look dazed, my sweet," I went on. "Are you hearing any of those messages from other dimensions which you told me about last night?"

Rhitha moved away from the tree and looked me full in the face. "Do you want me to be absolutely honest and frank?" she enquired.

"Of course," was the only thing I could say.

"Well, Gor darling, to tell you the truth, ever since we have been in this alley and near this tree I have been listening to a long rigmarole going on and on and on and on, defending this vivisection atrocity. O yes! and much more frightening than that, Gor darling, I have seen the face of the Being, far above us, up in the air, who has been talking to me."

"What sort of thing did he say?" I asked her.

"He said that there was only one important thing in life. He said that eating and drinking and building and painting and writing and carving and making music and racing and boxing and competing in athletics and having children and looking after them, were all only ways of amusing ourselves while we kept our race alive upon the earth. But he said that the one important thing, the one thing for which we were here, the one thing about which as human beings we had a right to be proud of, was our struggle to *understand*! Yes, he said the only important thing in life is to understand life; to understand what the earth and the ocean and the stars and every sort and condition of fire really and actually consisted of! And above everything else, he kept repeating, the important thing is to understand the nature of the creatures, lower in the scale than ourselves, who inhabit earth, air and water, and perhaps even fire; and in order to understand these creatures, their ways, their feelings, their bodily and mental reactions, it was absolutely essential to subject them to every kind of examination and experiment. We vivisectors, he said, do not do what we do in order to obtain for ourselves the curious satisfaction that is usually described as 'sadistic pleasure.' If such pleasure comes to us in pursuit of our duty, well! that is, if our temperament happens to be a sadistic one, what might be called, as the proverb says, 'virtue bringing its own reward.' But since the whole purpose of life is to understand life, it is absolutely essential that we should experiment with animals and with birds and with fishes; and although at present we have no idea where there are creatures who live in fire, we certainly must keep our attention fixed on fire so as not to miss them if they are there, and not to lose the opportunity of experimenting upon *them also*, if they exist."

Here, Rhitha stopped speaking; and I noticed the most extraordinary expression cross her features.

"Can you see this face up there now?" I enquired, not a little disconcerted by the strange look she had.

Rhitha nodded. And it was then that I cried out to

her: "O please, please, my dear, tell me what you see—tell me, tell me quick! Your face is so white!"

"Don't look at me, Gor. Look down at the ground. But hold my hand tight."

I obeyed her to the letter. On the ground I saw a small black ant carrying some object, smaller than itself, of a pale yellow colour, and followed by another ant, a little larger, that did not seem to be carrying anything.

"His face is like a vulture's. But it's his eyes that frighten me most. They seem to be saying to every worm and toad and lizard: 'You must let me take off your skin a little higher up please! I want to see exactly what's underneath it *there* and *there*. You say it hurts. O I never stop for *that*!' Then his eyes seem to scoop at the body of a dying rabbit. 'O no! no! I can't possibly let you give up the ghost yet. Do you still feel *that*? No? Or only a very little? I can't explain to you now why it is so important to me to know if you have any feeling left *there*—yes! Just there! Hurting's part of it. If it *didn't* hurt, you wouldn't wriggle. And if you didn't wriggle, how should I get on with all my knowing and understanding?' Then those terrible eyes seem to go further. Having dissected living birds and living fishes, the mind behind those eyes begins to hunt for some helpless planet! O Gor! Gor! It's drawing me up along with it now! It has things that pull you like the horny suckers of a devil-fish! And they can gouge and scrape and claw and delve! O Gor! Gor! He's after the moon now! He's got the rim of the moon in his fingers! He's struggling to nibble or gobble from out that perfect rondure a moonlight-bleeding, moonlight-oozing piece of moon-flesh! Listen, Gor darling, listen, I beg you! Do you hear that extraordinary noise? Like the sound we hear late at night sometimes, and call it the wind! But it's no more the wind than it is the moaning of the sea! It's the moon! But the moon now has stopped lamenting its loneliness in space as the only satellite of the earth. It's shrieking now! Yes, the moon is shrieking! It's a sound much worse than a wail of inconsolable sorrow! It's a clear, harsh, raw shriek, a shriek of jagged hurting! It's that little corner of the moon quivering with the pain of being grabbed at with the idea of tearing it and wrenching it from its mother, even if her silver flesh shrieks! O Gor! I just can't stand it! He hasn't managed to get that piece of the moon out yet! But he will. He will! I'm sure he will."

Watching Rhitha's face and listening to her words and looking at the moon, though I could hear nothing and see nothing, I began to be frightened. I told myself I mustn't, I mustn't, I mustn't let myself get scared! With all the grave authority I could assume, speaking in fact as if I were Math the son of Mathonwy, "Stop that! Stop that!" I cried.

"Stop *what*, Gor darling? What is it I must stop?"

"You must stop imagining yourself yielding an inch to that wretch. You must stop thinking we can't intervene. I *can* and I *will* intervene; and you shall help me in doing so."

My voice had taken on a tone that really was rather impressive. The girl was dominated by it and looked up at me as if she were awaiting something from me that would change the entire situation. And something did come. It came in the form of a word, or rather of three words, three short words, each an expressive monosyllable. "*Up and out!*" I cried. "*Up and out!*"

Rhitha could not have been more startled. Indeed I was startled myself at the effect of this cry of mine. The cry was wholly involuntary. It just rushed out of me. I hadn't the faintest prescience of it before it was in the air, and its challenge and the echoes of its challenge resounding among the gulfs and chasms of the mountains of that moon I was seeking to rescue. But neither of us had time now to listen to echoes. Where, in the name of Jehovah, where, in the name of Jove, where in the name of Zeus, were we? And then I knew. The hydrogen bombs of both East and West had been dropped in one wild mad, reckless orgy of universal destruction. Atomic science, as it had long threatened to do, had murdered the whole human race. We were both rendered unconscious at first in the shock of being carried so high into the air. But we were unhurt and we were side by side when the shock was over.

We found ourselves standing on a grassy plain the horizon of which stretched away into the sky in every direction. There were no flowers there, no trees, no bushes, no plants, no growths of any kind, no reeds, no rushes. There were only millions upon millions of grass-blades, all of them green as the greenest emeralds, only not in the least transparent. The sky surrounding this green plain was the greyest sky I have ever seen. Grey is a funny colour. Grey is a tricky colour. Grey is a mysterious colour. Grey is a ghostly colour. It is very rarely that in our ordinary life upon earth, whether we are in the New World or in the Old World, in the north or the south, in the east or the west that we see any perfect example of the colour grey. The sea is never grey. Lakes, rivers, estuaries are never grey. I mean they are not as grey as was this amazing sky surrounding this emerald-green undulating plain.

Rhitha and I looked at each other in dazed silence.

"Is this the piece of the moon, do you suppose, Gor?" she murmured, "that I watched that demon trying to scoop and gouge out?"

"No! I can't believe *that*, my darling. I would say it's some completely unknown satellite of this earth that revolves either much slower or much faster because it is so small; but whether faster or slower I'm not mathematical or astronomical enough to know. In fact, my sweet, it's a shame that a clever girl like you should be tied up with an old heavy-weather book-worm like me! I feel a mad desire to run in to the Blaenau public library, and get a few of the latest books on astronomy!"

"You mean," murmured Rhitha with just the faintest tinge of mischief in her smile, "those books about galaxies and nebulae; things of which I never hear mention without wondering why one of them ends with a Latin plural and the other with an English plural! Is that because a Latin plural means they can't ever stop going on, while an English plural means that we just don't know whether they stop or don't stop?"

"What do you exactly mean by 'stop'?"

"O, I don't *exactly* mean anything! But *you* tell me, my dear, whether the stars in the sky go on forever or come to an end?"

I struggled in my mind to remember what a certain book I had got out of the Blaenau public library had declared on this point: but all I could think of were the two expressions, firstly "an expanding universe," and secondly "background material."

"I suppose, my dear child," I began, anxious to prove to this lively girl that to the massive masculine intellect an "expanding universe" was as obvious a truth as that two and two make four and that the existence of "background material" was as certain as the fact that if you could get paper at the stationer's you could also get ink, "I suppose that scattered throughout all space there are invisible little atoms of matter that any fiery star or rushing meteorite enjoys snatching up as it plunges around and of course, as it does so, gets bigger and bigger and bigger, till it swells at last into a proper grown-up star from being at the beginning nothing but a poor little infantile asteroid, if that is the library word for a star that so far is only a toddler."

Rhitha positively clapped her hands for joy. Everything that was maternal in her sensitive little body pulsed and palpitated and pullulated with excitement to think of these little babies among stars growing up to take their place in an "expanding universe."

We were both silent for a while, gazing, neither gaily nor sadly, but in one of those fits of abstracted quiescence into which for its own wise purpose the body leads the mind, at our green island and its mysterious grey horizon.

But it was not long before the girl murmured: "Don't you find it hard to believe that there are no living people left in Asia, Africa, America, Australia and New Zealand? Surely, Gor dear, there must be a few left? A few infants in Africa and a few old men in Scotland?"

She was watching my face so intently that she must have known that my thoughts, whatever they were, were troubling me quite a good deal.

"What is it, Gor darling?" she asked.

"How quick you are, little one, to read my mind! Well, I'll tell you, honestly and exactly, what I was thinking just then. I was thinking what a thing it is that the whole of Nature, that is to say all that we know of the earth and the sea and the air, is full of hideous cruelty; and save for a few grass-eating and nut-eating and fruit-eating creatures, most of the denizens of earth, water, air, and possibly even fire, feed upon each other. What I had in my mind was simply this natural and obvious question. If to have what we call *Nature* at all—that is to say to have such an elaborately complicated, such a teeming and seething cosmos of living things, all struggling with one another and most of them devouring one another—we are compelled to accept, practically unchanged, the spectacle that life has given us, wouldn't it be wise if we men—the final product of this blind and mad confusion, in which we might say that only the vegetable world and the mineral world with whatever weird sorts of 'souls' their sub-animal substances contain, live a peaceful life—wouldn't it be wise, I say, if we men, making use of the philosophy and the science which in our bold challenge to all the gods that ever were or will be, we have invented for ourselves, if we men, I say, were to put a final end to the whole business? Wouldn't the best retort to the self-elevating worshippers of Man as God, as well as to the self-prostrating worshippers of God as Man, be simply and solely to obliterate at one stroke the whole of Creation? Then and then only and in that way alone would the brutal and blustering and blatant eulogists of this murderous life of ours be reduced to their proper place.

"Why are we—answer me *that*, angel of my heart!—why are we debarred from deciding that this confounded creation of life, by this Grand Inquisitor and Master Vivisector we call God, this life which the greatest of all philosophers maintains appears by the eternal processes of matter—why, I say, are we debarred from deciding that it is the opposite of a praiseworthy thing, that it is in fact a wicked and abominable thing, to allow this life to go on?"

Rhitha, who had been listening to my diatribe with what struck me as excited amusement, now enquired eagerly: "But Gor, darling, what will it be like when we have destroyed creation? Will *we* be destroyed with it? Will you and I, I mean, no longer be here? Or what will the world look like if we're still here, on this grass-green plain, with this grey horizon all round us? Will everything be black darkness? Will there be no green grass, no grey sky, no earth, no sun, no moon, no stars? What shall we——"

She was interrupted by the sudden appearance, bolt out of the sky in front of us, of an extraordinary-looking creature.

"Do you two know who I am?" it said, uttering the words in English, but with an accent totally different from that of any English person I have ever met. For some odd reason, though I would be totally unable to explain to myself when or where I had heard that funny word, the word "Geezish" came into my head; and a moment later the word "Coptic." I gazed at the monster who had asked us, speaking with this extraordinary accent, if we knew who it was; and then without a moment's hesitation, I leapt upon it as if it had been a wild beast who had defied me to mortal combat. For one flashing second before leaping upon it, I had the feeling that I gathered together all I was and every power I possessed. I felt as if I gathered my whole body, soul, spirit, intellect, reason, feeling, imagination, tightly together. I felt as if I used every member I possessed and every nerve I possessed fused together in one consolidated organism, and then leapt upon this creature. I suppose, in what they call a "spiritual" sense, I am habitually such a ferocious swallower of situations and environments and of all that I see round me, that when I leapt upon this creature, as if it embodied everything I saw at that moment, I was in that second an incarnation of so much vitality, that the Being I leapt upon had no alternative but to yield.

The queer-looking creature was indeed completely staggered and not a little scared.

In the shock of his consternation and discomforture he fell backwards into a crouching and humiliating position. And then as I knelt above him on our brief battlefield of green grass, I felt that in my blind rush of force I had sufficiently subjugated him to know how it would feel to have him absolutely and permanently at my mercy and at my disposal. Something at that moment said to me, "Don't obliterate this creature, for you never know how desperately one day you may need such a creature as a servant! But get him well under control, now that you've got him down, so that, having learnt his lesson, he won't resist you again!"

Thinking thus, I arranged the feverish and convulsive shakings I was giving this extraordinary-looking creature in a sufficiently uneven manner to enable it to think, if it wanted to think, in as detached a way as I was thinking myself at this moment.

"Every creature in Nature," I cried, "is being treated as I am treating you. O how much better it would be—wouldn't it? wouldn't it? wouldn't it?—if the whole of Nature could be destroyed at one stroke?"

"But surely, master of mine," the creature cried in his Coptic or rather in his Geezish accent, "you will get my considered opinion better if you let me go."

At those words, I did rise up from above his grotesque body, and I did leave him—I will say "him" and not "it" from now on—to follow his own devices.

And it was then that Rhitha wisely intervened. But her voice was so low that for a moment all I could hear was this creature saying again, over and over again, that the war between the East and the West of the world had destroyed the whole human race. But at last I heard Rhitha's words.

"Ask it," she whispered, "Gor darling, what its name is and whether it's got a wife, and, if it has, what *her* name is and *where* she is!"

It was obvious that my subdued antagonist had understood her words, for he lifted his head out of the grass and replied promptly and distinctly, using English, although a many-membered monster, just as I had used it, although a many-weapon'd Welshman.

"My name is Org and we were blown up from Easter Island and my wife's name is Asm and she comes from Ultima Thule. And if you'd like to see her——"

"O please tell him," cried Rhitha, "that we'd love——"

But there, before we could say a word, easily, lightly, airily helping her monster of a mate to whatever substitute for claws, or paws, or fins, or hooves, or pads, or leathery heels, this surprising creature used instead of feet, was Mistress Asm of Ultima Thule herself!

"Are these people," enquired Asm, "enemies or friends?"

"Isn't that a feminine question!" chuckled Org. But it was obvious that Asm had made some sign to him to do what was clearly one of the most difficult of all things for Org to accomplish, namely, "to pull himself," as our authorities love to say, "together." But he managed it somehow and it was certainly the queerest assortment of fish-scales and bird-feathers and slabs of rhino-hide and blobs of elephant-muscle and soft patches of deer-skin and slippery expanses of seal-skins and whale-like curvatures of walrus-skin that composed the bodily presence of our visitor from Easter Island.

"As if I could tell, my dear!" the creature answered. "How can anyone know friends from enemies at a glance? They are friends of the moon, that much I can tell you, for they are strongly against that World-Demon who nibbles at the edges of the moon when he's hungry; though why a famished devil shouldn't satisfy his hunger, like the rest of us, I fail to see."

It was then that I made one of the grandest speeches of my whole life. I began with an emphatic and purposeful gesture, indicating magisterially that not only was the Monster Org and his lady Asm to lie down on the grass, but that my own faithful Rhitha was to assume the same quiescent posture.

"Here are we," I commenced with a magnificently, comprehensive movement of both my arms. "Here are we, two pairs of living beings, with all those freakish, incalculable caprices of imagination, emotion, pity, indignation, and amusement, which our various ancestors have possessed for thousands of years. How much more you two, of whom we know nothing but your names, are acquainted with the nature of life than I and my Rhitha are it is impossible for me to say; but if you are more enlightened in these matters than we are, the fact remains that there are limits to your knowledge, however extensive it is, and there must be a point in your accumulation of wisdom, as there is a point in our smaller amount, where all wisdom abruptly ends. Here we are, therefore, four beings alone in space, standing upon some sort of small satellite from which no doubt, when this grey sky turns black and when we grow aware of the glittering stars, we shall find ourselves surrounded by other consciousnesses similar to, or at least parallel with, our own. 'Long live Rhitha!' will then be my war-cry into space and 'Long live Asm!' will be yours. But O my dearer than strange pair of dedicated companions"—I became more and more of an orator as I went on—"don't you see that the important thing for us, who are the last living remnants of all the creatures that these old galaxies have spawned in their motley-whirling phantom-twirling nightmare-swirling neutron-hurling dance through space, is to make one supreme initial effort to ensure with absolute certainty that there shall be no more of this devilish creation of living things! I tell you this is our one grand last chance to achieve this desirable purpose! That much is proved by my precious Rhitha's shudder just now, when she saw that that desperately hungry cosmic demon had reached such a point of insatiable craving for food that he was actually nibbling at the margin of the moon! She shuddered at such a sight, as well she might; but she did not realize that it was a clear sign that the whole order of our old universe had run down like a worn-out and rusty clock; and that the time had come for us to take this blasted clock entirely out of the blundering hands of Zeus and Jupiter and Jehovah—and take it to pieces in fact!—'and remould it,' as some gipsy-minstrel expressed it the other day, 'nearer to the heart's desire.'"

Here I made a dramatic pause. But very soon—for, by the help of my infancy among the wandering sheep and restless orphans of Blaenau, I knew better than anyone between the sun and the moon how to handle both herds and herdsmen—very soon I saw the Ciceronian necessity, in the act of concluding my oration, of striking a completely different note. And thus, very slowly, and with an absolutely inspired manipulation of my shadow, I proceeded to strike this note, which was simply and solely one of deep, indrawn—and by this I mean that I, the speaker, drew magnetically into me the souls of all my three listeners—of deep indrawn *silence*; and with this I closed my oration.

This dramatic silence of mine, was, as I am always trying to make clear to the Simple Simons who know nothing of the noblest art in the world, far the most impressive way by which I could possibly have ended.

I had already noticed, though there was no sign of any sun up there, that shadows showed an unmistakable tendency to fall, though where the devil they came from, heaven itself, I am sure, couldn't have said.

Org was now sitting up in a rather curious position, considering the multiplicity of the members with which providence—or the process of evolution or the cruelty of vivisectionists—had endowed him; whereas both the ladies were lying gracefully and even seductively on that beautiful green grass.

It now became quite clear to me, from obvious signs, that as Org contemplated our two ladies on the grass he was unable to restrain, grotesque monster though he was, both a lecherous desire for those lovely limbs, and also, I could see this for myself in his expression, a real, deep, exquisite delight in the bewitching and sometimes almost miraculous grace that the bodies of women can assume when a real opportunity occurs. Are they, I asked myself, ever as completely unconscious of their physical beauty as I am sometimes completely unconscious of my power of oratory? Well! At any rate these two particular expressions of our life upon earth, my oratory and their beauty, had been brought to a climax by my dramatic silence, aided by this more than dramatic, this almost supernatural shadow, which had suddenly descended out of space to aid me, completely unimpelled by any thrower of shadows of which I was aware. This dramatic silence of mine, aided by this space-fallen shadow, was perhaps more Roman than Greek. What I hope I resembled was the culminating subsidence of one of Cicero's most resounding sentences; and I would like to think of it too as not very different from one of those thunder-claps of conclusive finality in a poem of Catullus. But whatever it resembled it had an effect totally unlike my anticipated effect. The whole landscape in which Rhitha and I and Org and Asm had been resting now commenced a palpable movement of its own. It began to swerve, it began to tilt sideways, it began to circulate through the air as though propelled by its own volition. It began to make the most beautifully undulating gyrations. And, as the ground beneath us rose, the colour of the grass completely changed. As I watched it I imagined it was changing to blue but I may very easily have been misled by the peculiar effect that rapid motion can have upon grass-blades. What I took for blue might have much more properly been described as steel-grey. At any rate it was changing, even now as I looked round. But whatever was happening to the colour of the grass, it was not long before we two pairs of bewildered earthlings found ourselves in an unusually dark night, but exposed to the peering eyes of more stars than any of us had ever seen directed towards the earth! I don't know what the others thought, but what I wondered in my heart was how it was possible for so many orbicular rondures to exist, as they apparently were existing, quite harmoniously side by side, moving in predetermined curves round and about one another and not attacking each other with supernatural ferocity, or trying to cut each other in pieces or to swallow up each other dead or alive! The females of our little party did indeed find themselves very quickly absorbed in a lively argument as to exactly where among all the magnificent hieroglyphics drawn so perfectly across the blackness of the sky was the star familiarly known as "the North Star." Rising on one of his feet or paws or fins, Org begged me so say something.

"Yes, yes, brother," I responded, "the moment has indeed come for you and me to show the mettle of our sex! As for the whereabouts of the North Star we can let that go: but the moment has come for us to announce and declare a world-shaking revolution, worthy of real thinkers and of such intellects as inaugurate the great changes that convulse and remould the history of the world. Will you allow me, Brother Org, to speak for us both as I address our attentive if somewhat simple-minded ladies?"

Org nodded with his biggest-land-snout and at the same time winked with his smallest sea-eye.

But never had any empire-builder in history to decide more rapidly what his world-policy was than I had to do at that moment. I expect all such cosmogonic decisions, if we knew the truth, have been dictated by just the same sort of small personal irritation as mine was at that moment. I expect Moses and Joshua and Pericles and Caesar and Alexander and Gustavus Adolphus and Napoleon and General Gordon all made the most momentous decisions of their lives when it came to the point by reason of some grotesquely little prick or sting or hurt or pique or minute stab of human vexation, caused in many cases by the simplest and absurdest misunderstanding. I will not go quite so far as to say that my sublimely tragic decision was taken purely for such a reason; but I will say that the emotional force I threw into it was accentuated by the fact that the fondness my Rhitha had been lately displaying for Org's seductive Asm had been causing me several throbs of obscure resentment.

"Our political revolution," I now declared in a majestically judicial tone worthy of Rhadamanthus himself, "and it must be remembered that we represent all the creatures in earth, water, air, and fire, and in their name we—that is to say Org and his lady Asm and I and my lady Rhitha—do hereby renounce and revoke, in one desperate and final reversion, all the claims of our jungle, of our sea, of our forest, of all the levels of life in the teeming margins between land and water! Yes, we renounce, I say, and revoke and reject forever all the claims of the living multitudes of swarming creatures that the power we call Nature engenders, the claims of worms and slugs, the claims of toads and frogs, the claims of newts and tadpoles, the claims of moles and badgers and foxes, the claims of rats and mice, the claims of stags and deer, the claims of every insect that crawls and of every insect that flies, and of all the insects that neither crawl nor fly! Yes, we have come, Org and I, as representatives of all these weak and helpless creatures; but we have also come as representatives of all the powerful and ravening creatures, of lions and tigers, of leopards and panthers, of elephants and hippos, of crocodiles and rhinos, of rattlesnakes and vipers, of gorillas and chimpanzees; and we have also come as representatives of every bird in the air and every fish in the sea! Yes, and not only these! We include in our grand refusal all the half-lives of the mosses and lichens and the most hidden and secretive funguses of the woods and the most recondite sea-weeds of the depths of the ocean! Yes, we four, we two males and we two females, are now speaking for all the four-thousand billions of living creatures in the entire universe. And we are announcing to the said universe that, from this moment we and the whole mass of lives we represent do proclaim and declare that we are withdrawing from the whole horrible and appalling play; yes, we have decided to refuse henceforth to bring to life one single offspring more to breathe this cruel and anguishing air and to live this iniquitous and abominable life! I tell you, we four, who represent all these mysterious multitudes, have decided on their behalf that from now on, all life, in all places and under all conditions is going to end!"

It was then that Rhitha and Asm ceased disputing about the North Star. It was clear to my exalted pride that they had been stirred in the very depths of their hearts by my powerful words; and the thought rushed through my mind that it was a real touch of the true genius of a master orator that, at that perilous moment when I had to decide just what my world-policy was, I decided upon annihilation rather than upon creation and upon suicide rather than upon any form of reconstruction. O how much easier it is, I now clearly saw, to attack than to defend, and to advocate destruction than to indicate the faintest possibility of restoration! Yes, both our wives now rose up on the tips of their toes and stretched their long slender white arms upward, and with their lovely bodies quivering with excitement turned their heads towards the stars, just as I had done myself with the gesture of an invincible orator while I shrieked my challenge to whatever appalling power it was, a power far worse than the old Homeric "anangké" or "necessity," that was driving us willy-nilly to increase with our wretched little quota the horrible enormity of life's tangled chaos.

But still upon us four living beings those millions upon millions of blazing stars gazed down with contemptuous casual, careless and sardonic amusement. The resonant cry that I had just now flung among those mocking points of glittering contempt was now reinforced by the silent cries of Rhitha and Org and Asm; and what I found of curious interest in my incurable introspection was the fact that neither I nor they—no! not one of us pitifully stirred-up four persons—had had the faintest idea to *whom* or to *what* we were addressing our "Declaration of Independence" and our right to end life instead of helping it to go on, and announcing our resolution to bring the whole damned business to an end. But now—and it all came in a moment—I *knew* to whom and to what we were making these universal proclamations. For *there*, straight before us, and straight above us, as our swirling and swivelling and swinging and slithering and slanting and shimmering little satellite revolved in its resolutely directed curves, was nothing less than Time Itself! Yes it was to Time Itself that I had been proclaiming my desire that all we creatures of the elements and sons and daughters of nature should perish once and for all at one stroke and never, no! not any of us, appear again! Yes, it was to Time Itself that I had been praying that all the children of Time might perish forever! Vacuum vacuo! Nihil super nihil! And *what* a monster Time was, thus envisaged, as we encountered it now! And all the while around it, as well as around us, were those millions of glittering little peering eyes! But what had become of the huge genial bonfire-furnace of a life-giving star that we have always been accustomed to call the sun? Clean gone forever, had he? And what had happened to our sweet sorceress the moon, upon whose enchanted flesh Rhitha had caught that unspeakable demon nibbling? Gone also forever had she too?

But what did I hear then? Did I hear one of those tiny twinklers in the distance, shining atoms, baby sparks, crowding out of space to attend the death-bed of Great-Aunt Time? Did I hear one of them—from the Pleiades, was it?—starting to cry? To confess the truth, little far-away fire-flies, I began to feel a trifle funny myself: but funny or not, I was going to play now the part of the bell that tolls the twelve-o'clock death-notes of Time!

I could see that Org was affected, just as I was, by the appearance of this incredible Monster directly before us, which he knew, as well as I knew, was nothing less than Time Itself.

The terrifying enormity in the sky to which we were getting so close, although in any scientific calculation it must have been about half way to the nearest star, was certainly a horrible object.

In the frantic circular cleavings of the dark air, made by our platter-shaped field of green grass, the nearer we approached to the thing called Time, the more clearly did we see that it resembled an enormous black slug. It was not exactly in every detail like a slug. It had very large eyes for instance, and out of its mouth wavered, explored, fumbled, groped, a very flexible forked tongue. No doubt my powers of observation are very limited, but somehow I find it hard to associate either big eyes or forked tongues with black slugs. This is not from ignorance of these creatures, for I used invariably to encounter them in my morning walks into the valley called Cwm Bowydd in my early days at Blaenau. No, I shall never forget to the end of my life this extraordinary ascent of ours; for here were Org and I mounting up with the rough, genial, good temper of a pair of sporting pals, while our girls as they ascended with us had the very look, awed, grave, abstracted, exalted, absorbed, of *two* Virgin Marys undergoing the mystical experience of Assumption.

You must understand that our two ladies were really so beautiful that they would have made a perfect subject for one of the great, old, religious painters, such as Titian, or Tintoretto, or Giorgione, or El Greco; though it would have needed a touch from Goya perhaps, or even from the more modern imagination of Gustave Doré, to do justice to this mystery-monster that was the true image of Time.

As we approached this monstrous thing, with the gliding, tilting, slanting, curving, sliding, switching motion of our unusual vessel, I could see those bottomless eyes of his advancing, receding, extending, distending, revealing indeed, so it seemed to me, such an interior cavern of nerve-passages and such a labyrinth of glandular ducts, and such a convoluted gallery of shudder-causing orifices, that you felt that, if once the news actually reached here of such a stupendous mouthful, as a raging, roaring, ramping, roving biped from Blaenau of the male sex, the whole interior anatomy of this man-eating minotaur would explode from greedy joy and blow up, strewing that little corner of the void with the scoriac soot of a whole crater of masculine life-illusion!

But what I had to do now was to keep repeating to myself the rending, cleaving, splitting, and splintering cry of my original challenge: "No more of this blasted procreation! No more of the swarming legs and arms and hairs and bristles of these jostling by-blows of Time!"

We must, I think, have been dangerously near the bursting-point of some sort of explosion, when, all in a moment I heard the voice of Org uttering a warning cry. O, what a jealous pang shot through me when I heard him, for why had not I been the one to cry "halt!" at this juncture?

Yes, I heard Org cry out in a shrill high-pitched reverberating voice: "All eyes to the left!"

We all instantaneously obeyed him of course; and there, lo! right before us, piercing the very heart of the Time-Monster, ran a gaping tunnel, quite big enough for our vessel with all four of us on board, to pass through, and revealing the fact that not only were we heading clear through the repulsive and revolting body of Time, but that our vessel had already done something of much more importance.

What it had done was to cut into two halves a delicate, sensitive vital gland in the centre of the Time-slug's midriff, which now was floating, draggled and loose, and dripping with enormous drops of blood, completely clear of the diaphragm to which it had belonged.

As our vessel emerged huge shadows of the murdered body of the Slug of Time moved round us, each one a little different from the others but all anxious to escape from our presence in any possible direction. And then we noticed that the whole blazing mass of the stars above our heads, of the stars above the head of the dead body of Time, of the stars above all the heads, human, sub-human, or superhuman, in the advancing, or retreating, enlarging, or diminishing, expanding, or receding universe had vanished. Yes! There, before us, clear through the body of Time was the ultimate Void. But the Void was not empty. In the Void there was still Eternity. We had passed through that tremendous tunnel into nothingness only to be faced by something worse.

But do you know what just then was my greatest comfort and relief? Dare I confess it? Nothing less than to have done forever and a day with the stars! No more of these confounded galaxies and nebulæ of an expanding universe! No universe at all! No multiverse either! Just simply *Nothing*.

It was wonderful enough being carried through the belly of Time, but it was more wonderful still, in fact it was something beyond words to all four of us, when we saw—for none of us thought of eternity—into what heavenly expanse our ship was conveying us!

It was carrying us, not only through Time's despoiled diaphragm, but actually through the whole vast atmosphere that surrounds the idea of Time; and we all told ourselves that we should be free from every landscape, seascape, airscape, firescape, that submitted to Time's domination.

Into such freedom, into such liberty, into such inexpressible escape our circular boat, our coracle from Wales, finally carried us! No more the greyness of ocean around us! No more the dazzlingness of immeasurable star-points above us, no more the blind, dumb, dense, opaque mass of earth-matter beneath us! Yes, we were free of the whole thing! We were floating in an immensity without any up or down, or right or left, or high or low! But O! how difficult I now find it to convey to the future decipherer of this log-book of mine what we all four felt when our vessel suddenly ceased to make any definite movement at all, either forward or backward, but began slowly and casually and yet quite carelessly and indifferently, turning round and round on her own axis! But why did she do this? For no other reason than the simple and absurdly obvious one that we were free of Time, we passengers on Gor Goginog's ship, G.G. Time Destroyer. We had all the time assumed—note how I bring in Time over its very corpse—that we were now free to take our ease in complete disregard of any rules, laws, systems, methods or directions from any power or from any quarter, whether in the heavens above or in the earth beneath that didn't suit the whims, wishes and inclinations of our irresponsibility. But apparently we had been making, all four of us, incredible fools of ourselves! For we were now confronted by something far more mysterious than Time and far more dominant than Time. In plain words we were now confronted by Eternity.

I don't know what my nature-created, vivisection-distorted rival, Org, felt, or what either of our girls felt, but I can assure you I said to myself at once: "Now my Gor, this is a real test for you: probably the greatest you will ever have in your time. And what I want you to do is to watch and observe and examine everything you see; and avoid if you possibly can, any form or kind of action that is not implicit in your being just what you are and observing everything you can!"

What struck me first, and this did indeed impress and amaze me, was the fact that the sight of Eternity was the sight of a repulsive, disgusting, sickly, unpleasant, disagreeable thing. What I expected to see; but with my strong predilection for painting above all the other arts and my instinctive association of all I valued in life with my sense of sight, I found it amazing that when confronted at last with this terrific ultimate thing, I found nothing in its appearance that impressed me at all; in fact I found nothing in its appearance that I could possibly describe; not because it was beyond description, but because it was beneath description. As a thing to look at, as a thing to see, Eternity was pitifully unimpressive and woefully unappealing.

It was not exactly, at least not to my sight, colourless; for I had my own fixed idea as to what colourlessness was, namely a pale grey like the greyness that surrounded the edge of the flat, round, quoit-shaped meadow upon which we were still travelling. Eternity, as I saw it now, was like a dirty-yellowish-ivory-white vapour interpenetrating the pallid murkiness of any ordinary dreary day and suffusing the tedious duskiness of any ordinary cloudy night. The Thing's presence in the darkness was immediately made known to me by a sense quite different from the sense of sight; namely by the sense of sound. And the sound I now heard emerging from this monstrous-shaped, corpse-coloured vapour, floating about in the black darkness of night, was the most horrible sound that can possibly be imagined. It was a low distinct sucking sound, followed by a gulping and a gurgling. In fact it was the sound of swallowing on a scale too huge and horrible even to be called superhuman; and after a second's pause there came a gastric rumble, mingled with a chuckle of revolting self-glorification, as if the swallower couldn't commend itself enough for having got its victim where, in sublime satisfaction, it could begin the process of digesting what it had successfully swallowed.

What I now began to realize for the first time was the unfathomable depth of the self-satisfaction of Eternity. How often, I told myself—and O! how I longed to tell it to the filthy vapour of the colour of dirty toilet-paper that now surrounded us!—have we been fooled by the seductively awful and deceptively appalling aura which so many pious tricksters have thrown round the word "Eternity," in order to scare us about the fate of our souls! They have long tried to drive the more sensitive among us insane by this holy trick; and indeed in certain cases, as in that of the poet Cowper, they have, to their intense delight, succeeded.

"And the worst of it is," so my thoughts ran on, "many eloquent and inspired writers, such as Carlyle and Ruskin and even the self-possessed and sensible Mr. Emerson, have added their quota of nonsensical adoration before the foul-smelling throne of this arch-illusion. Ordinary people have been perpetually fooled by this stinking humbug; for let it be, from now on," so I decided in my heart, "thoroughly recognized and understood that this solemn and holy thing, Eternity, is just so much rubbish and balderdash. As for the death of Time, *that* is only like a faithful old staircase-clock having run down. It may give us a momentary sadness, as if we yielded to a sigh of sympathy when a tired old horse that had been pulling our cart up hill for a mile stopped to rest, but this poppycock claim of Eternity, this bloated, blown-up soap-bubble of sham awfulness, cleverly concocted by our priests and rhetoricians to make us ordinary folk—babies as we are when it comes to such things!—stand hushed and trembling in silent reverence, this is a completely different story."

As you've detected by this time, you who are reading the log-book of G.G.Time-Destroyer, I'm neither a very brave man nor a very wise man; but I am one to blurt out the truth both about myself and about what I see. So at this moment, when I realized the loathsome nature of this cloud of vapour from all the scavengers' carts and all the mortuary trestles and all the hospital cess-pools in the world, I became seized with such blind fury at the humbug we human simpletons had listened to for so long, that I could no longer contain myself, but from the deck, so to speak, of our whirling, swirling green-grass vessel I deliberately spat—yes! I spat three times—into the face of Eternity: and after doing so I cried out to this reverent swallower of honest men's corpses: "I can clearly see now, you dirty, sickly-yellow, blood-sucking devourer of heroic lives, that you are nothing but the master-sham of the universe! I tell you now that the smallest living insect swallowed by you is far more god-like than you are! Who created you, I would like to know? Not great Jehovah, the formless, shapeless, nameless God of Israel! Not great Zeus, the son of Kronos, the cloud-ruling, thunder-wielding God of the ancient Greeks! Not great Jupiter, the all-powerful God of the Romans, celebrated in Blaenau by the utterance 'Iau' every Thursday, the day we Saxons associate with our thundering Thor! I'll tell you, you dirty, filthy, sickly-yellow humbug, you who pretend that you've got a position greater than the Garden of Eden, greater than Mount Olympus, and greater than the Pantheon of Rome, I'll tell you who created you! A set of cunning, cruel, mean, avaricious, greedy, crafty priests who called themselves priests of Jesus! But in reality they were anything but that. Jesus was a wise man, a good man, a godlike man, and a miraculous healer of the sick. And they also call themselves, these cunning teachers, disciples of Paul of Tarsus. But in reality they were and are anything but that. Paul was one of the greatest and most inspired men who have ever lived. His ideas were not their ideas nor was his talk their talk. Yes these priests who used the names of Jesus and Paul to support their lies invented Eternity so as to bribe us with Heaven and frighten us with Hell. Yes! you unnecessary horror! It is your priests and prelates and rulers and spiritual false prophets—in fact those very Scribes and Pharisees that Jesus was always denouncing!—who are the ones who invented you! Help me, Org! Help me, help me! I begin to feel I shall soon be overcome by this nauseating vapour! O we must all help each other! We must! We must!

"If we don't, we'll all be swallowed up by this curst Eternity's loathsome, gurgling, stinking, leprous, filthy gullet, this voracious maw that these priests and pastors and elders and inquisitors and prelates and literary rhetoricians have piled up in the clear, clean, beautiful Void! So you must, you *must* help me, Org! And tell your lovely little Asm that she must help us as Rhitha is helping now! Then there'll be at least two males and two females, fresh from the old Earth, who refuse to be awed by this everlasting lie! Don't you see, Rhitha dearest, don't you see, Asm, this monster is infinitely worse than that Old Slug through whose bloody heart we've got here! Think, Org, my boy, what has happened to all the other inhabitants of the Earth! Where are the millions of East India? Where are the billions of China? What has become of all the black Africans? Where are the French? the Germans? the Italians? the Spaniards? Have these atomic explosions really destroyed the whole human race? Are we four really the only specimens who are left alive? Well, there it is! I've always hoped the whole lot of us would soon be done for; and now it's come! Or hasn't it come? Answer me, Org! Answer me!"

Org answered me in the manner that was best suited to his multiform and composite structure. He rose up on one of his hairy legs and heaved towards me two walrus-like shoulders, as well as what might well have been the hump of an unknown sub-oceanic camel. As for the lovely little Asm, she leapt up on the very top of Org's grotesque back, a leap that made her bewitching hips quiver and shake in delicious concord with the undulations of her sylph-like thighs. My own precious Rhitha kissed one hand after the other as she waved her white arms towards me, while her siren-like hair floated on the sickly vapour about us so gracefully that its heavenly curves completely redeemed all the loathsome mist they invaded.

"Do you think, Org," I asked him; "Do you think, Asm?" I asked her; "Do you think, Rhitha, that if we all four danced a dance of gay erotic defiance clear into the heart of this horrible mist, crying out as we do so any ribald nonsense that comes into our heads, some randy catch such as, 'Let Eternity stew in its own bloody juice,' while we hug one another *sans* shame or excuse, till the hulking great horror be driven to croon, 'I'll be dancing myself if this doesn't stop soon!'"

"Yes, Gor! Yes, Gor! Yes, Gor!" they all three replied with one voice; and, led by me—for I'm a perfect leader of any crazy crew—in a few seconds, there we all four were turning head over heels, and ballet-bouncing backwards and forwards, and leaping on each other's shoulders, and making little acrobatic towers of ourselves right in the middle of Holy Eternity!

But it suddenly came over me that there must be a yet more scandalous way of conveying to this preposterous monster our discovery that all this hushed and awful solemnity, all this cringing and reverential gravity, all this watchful and altar-facing expectancy, all this thaumaturgical silence, all this heavily-charged aura of factitious worship, is nothing more than an aerial fossil, a sort of huge liquidated ammonite or porous signature of Ammon, printed, not upon clay or stone, but upon the air itself, and printed on the air thousands upon thousands of years ago, before mankind had come to realize to what this life of theirs really amounted, this pinched and prodded, this poked and pampered, this festered and pestered life, concerning the creation of which there has been far too much fuss. Yes, what came into my head now was that we four entities, remnants of a race who had decided that in any case it was time for them to disappear, ought to have the simple wit, since we were already mocking and fooling this factitious Eternity instead of bowing and scraping before it, the simple wit to invent some more palpable way of showing this monster what our opinion of him was.

"Let's scrabble," I growled to my three companions in a furious undertone, as we jogged up and down through the vaporous aura of this obnoxious minotaur, "in the grass of our landscape-ship for some horse-dung and cattle-dung and sheep's turds and birds' droppings, and when we've filled our pockets with these wholesome missiles, let us give Eternity a good pelting with them! And if you protest 'To what end and purpose are we to do this?' I reply 'Just purely and simply to make the Monster created by these Holy Cringers and Holy Suckers realize our contempt for him!'

"Yes. O yes, my dears," I went on as I began grubbing in the grass of our green field that was now behaving very queerly and revolving on its edge like a circling and spinning quoit, "pick up all this hard gravel and all the soft mud and all the bits of sheep's dung and birds' dung you can get hold of, and we'll rush into the heart of this sanctified Erebos and hear the sod gulp and gurgle! We'll teach this great Bugaboo to reduce its pretensions! We'll teach it that the humblest insect measuring out its miserable days by the pug-wuggery and skull duggery of the old Slug of Time is worth far more than this defecating bubble! Be careful as you tread on its oily fog-navel, my friends, for we don't want to fall thumping back on our green field! But it just shows what a humbug the thing is that we're able to tread on it at all! O, you're so silent and hushed and holy and hoary, aren't you, you herpeton of hypocrisy! And we must all count one-two-three correctly, mustn't we, if we're not to fizzle forever and ever? Yes! We've got to confess, have we, that the number four leads nowhere because it stays where we've put it, but the number three rolls and rolls and rolls till, by being all and nothing at the same time, it proves the existence of Eternity! And then we learn that where Eternity exists all natural things and all natural feelings perish! No living creature can look upon that sickly, sticky, ivory-yellow vapour without loathing it and no living creature can approach it without knowing perfectly well how it longs to make us part of it. All that is Something it turns into Nothing! Eternity is the big hole that connects being with not-being. Its chief love is to suck down all that shivers at the sight of it! See how it gloats now over your fear and my fear of being swallowed up! It knows how we'd sooner cling to any straw rather than let it devour us. But you wait! you monster! You wait, you hideous disgusting horror! We'll teach you to be yourself! We'll show you what Eternity really is!

"Yes, we'll show you the very last thing you ever thought to see, namely your contemptible self! Eternity-Scum! Eternity-Scurf! Eternity-Stink! Eternity, the filthiest lie ever to pass out of the anus of the Nonsense-doll! I tell you, you sticky, yellow, swollen monster, we four living things will turn you back into what you once were, which is a secret you think known only to those who invented you! But it is a secret we know. And you shall know we know it! You think you are an indispensable background to all living things. But that's where you go wrong. We four living creatures have reached you by passing through the heart of Time. Time is dead. And now *you* are going to die. You think Eternity cannot die. *That* is the conceit that makes you swell and swell and swell. But Eternity *can* die, and you are even now, though you don't know it, a dying monster!"

Thus I cried in a transport of triumph; but I never for one moment dreamed how the end would really come about; the actual end of this terrifying Eternity, that has been used by Religion for so long to frighten mankind into lick-spittling servitude. But its end came now; and came about purely and simply from its own disgusting greediness. For no sooner were we all four clear of the unspeakable horror, than do you know, O lucky posterity, what the monster did? It actually bent down, and after opening a hole in itself as wide as the Milky Way, it deliberately swallowed the dead body of Time! Yes, it swallowed it whole, just as the preachers had threatened us with being swallowed! And it was this swallowing of the corpse of Time that finished Eternity. The thing's whole vaporous covering turned in a second inside out. And beneath *that* covering another covering turned inside out. And after this process, which was desperately shocking to witness had gone on for several minutes—lo and behold! the thing had, so to speak, turned its very self inside out; in other words, *had swallowed itself*. And there before us, where Eternity had been, was simply a hollow void. The big black hole between being and not-being was gone.

We were still standing, all four of us, upon our familiar grassy landscape—though perhaps I ought not to describe Org's straddling upheaval as "standing"—when suddenly our two lovely ladies, for Asm was nearly as beautiful as Rhitha, seized each other by the hands, and, with their long white arms outstretched, pointed excitedly upward at the vast, endless, dark, unencumbered space that now surrounded us on all sides.

"Do you see who's coming, Org?" cried Asm. "Do you see who's coming, Gor?" cried Rhitha.

"O who? O who? my dears!" Org and I murmured with one voice, bewildered and puzzled and awestruck.

"Mathonwy," answered our ladies. "Mathonwy! Lord of all the sea-coasts of the World!"

Org and I stared at each other in amazement.

"There! There! There! *There!*" And our ladies, still clutching each other's hand, pointed to a majestic little statue of a formidably bearded monarch made of delicate porcelain, standing upright upon a china pedestal and moving rapidly through the air, pedestal and all, with as much assurance as our grassy landscape itself was displaying as it carried us up and out. And then I suddenly knew what they meant and who it was who had come. It was an image, if not himself, of the oldest of all our native Welsh gods, the father of Math of Caer Dathyl.

"Mathonwy!" cried our two ladies, "Mathonwy! Mathonwy!" they repeated in an ecstasy of delight, clasping each other's hands as if they'd been sisters all their days and had clung to each other for support from infancy!

"But is he a real person?" I asked. "Perhaps he's only an ornament thrown away by some child in heaven!" Org suggested.

"No! No! No!" cried Rhitha and Asm with one voice: "It's Mathonwy! It's Mathonwy!"

"But that figure trailing along on a pedestal isn't alive!" cried Org. "He's a china statue, and only a little one at that!"

I couldn't help adding: "And he can't walk with his legs as we all can! He just has to be carried through the air on a marble pedestal, as if he'd come from the British Museum."

But neither Org's commonsense nor my mockery could quell the obsession in the breasts of our ladies. They continued to swing their clasped hands backwards and forwards, as if rocking an invisible baby in an angelic cradle; and as the porcelain monarch on his pedestal drew near, our girls seemed to lose their heads completely and began bowing and scraping before him in the most approved manner, and repeating over and over, as if they were using at one and the same time consecrated Latin and sacramental Greek, "Mathonwy have mercy upon us! Mathonwy save us! O Lord God of the Ancient Britons! Save us and help us we humbly implore thee!"

And as the pedestal'd figure came quite close to us and as I gazed intently at this mysterious monarch's face, and as I remembered how his son, Math of Caer Dathyl, had created a girl for Llew Llaw Gyffes out of the flowers of the oak and the flowers of the broom and the flowers of the meadow-sweet, it suddenly rushed into my head that, when the poet of poets hints in his casual fashion that there are more things in heaven and earth than our, or anybody else's philosophy dreams of, he may have met—for it is clear enough that Welshmen tickled his fancy and that when he did meet them he humoured them to the limit—

one of their race, who, like myself, indulged a mania for idolatry to such an extreme that what you might call his "household gods" were collected from every country on this planet.

I would dearly have liked to have been able to boast that the moment my eyes met those of the mysterious Father of Math we exchanged a look of absolute understanding; but that would be a lie beyond even me, for this ancestral Brythonic deity took not the faintest personal interest in any of us. Indeed he glanced away from us very much as an absorbed entomologist who was making a special study of Green Hairstreaks might turn listlessly away from a couple of pairs of ordinary Meadow Browns.

"Are you people," he enquired, throwing less interest into his tone than if he'd been asking us where in this Void was the nearest lavatory, "going north, or south, or east, or west, or are you perhaps thinking of settling down up here and are anxious to know the price, in ducats or drachmas or thalers or rupees or roubles, of a small acreage in space?"

I noticed with astonishment that, no sooner had this floating image of prehistoric sovereignty arrived close to us, than the preposterous ancient thus pedestal'd in his absurd pomp started to make lewd and lecherous leers at both our ladies. But if I was astonished at this I was still more amazed by its effect.

Both my Rhitha and Org's Asm became a couple of austere and icy little statues of outraged virtue; and in less than a second this porcelain poppet of presumption was transformed from a prehistoric divinity into a negligible pimp, and ordered abruptly to go to hell. And to hell, or to somewhere equally unprepossessing, Mathonwy in his humiliation would certainly have gone, if a new apparition had not descended at our side upon the flat expanse of our grass-green world-ship. This was nothing less than the star Aldebaran, surrounded by a great wheel of incredibly coloured lights. We all, including our lewd little Welsh god from those prehistoric days when monarchs were allowed as many wives and concubines as they could afford, were struck dumb with awe and wonder. Mathonwy murmured and we all repeated after him, just as if we had been children at school, the word "Aldebaran." And then Aldebaran assumed control of the whole situation. Stars of this magnitude, perhaps all stars, after existing for a few thousand million years, acquire the power of communicating with other consciousnesses, no matter the distance between them; and of conveying intelligible meaning without the use of words. Thus having admitted freely to us his identity, this wonderful denizen of space proceeded at once, without any ceremony, to disclose to us the reason for its coming among us. The personal appearance of our starry visitor was less overwhelming than a person would have anticipated. As we now looked at him, Aldebaran presented the appearance of a wheel of white lights, lights not very close to each other, but some of them, although still enduringly white, shot through by gleaming rays of coloured flame. It was these flames that struck me as being quite supernatural in their hypnotic power. Aldebaran's first words, after he had made his polite obeisance to us all as a group, were addressed to Mathonwy.

"Well, master," he said, and the richly coloured lights in the broad wheel of his personality shone more and more lustrously as his wordless words entered the skull of the porcelain-headed tyrant at which they were aimed, "You and I have known each other for quite a number of these little pegs of time that our young friends here call centuries; but whether we shall go on knowing each other for an equal number of them I don't feel quite sure; though I daresay, if we both decided we wanted to, we would."

Then, with a subtlety of politeness that I never dreamed could possibly exist among the stars, he caused the marvellous wheel of his being to turn on its invisible axis just about half of all the way round; with the result that the deepest-coloured of those incredible lights, whose appearance in some queer way—whether due to the clown in me or to the blasphemer in me, for I suspect I contain both—put me in mind of the descent of the Third Person of the Trinity upon the pathetic craniums of the twelve apostles, shone now more directly and more warmly on us than on the despotic little figure of Mathonwy floating about on his pedestal.

"Well, my dear earthlings," Aldebaran began, while he indicated in a gentle undertone that conveyed to our minds, not before and not after the rest of what he said, but curiously parallel or concurrent with it, that it would be nice if we all sat down in a wide circle on the grass; a stellar hint which all four of us obeyed at once, while Mathonwy was left with no alternative, since the starry wheel was turning in the centre of us, save to pedestal it as best he could round the outside of our circle.

"What I've come to tell you," Aldebaran went on, "is that all of us stars, together with all our companions in all the gulfs and abysses of Space—and I beg you to note, my young friends, that this applies to all the astronomical bodies, such as, they tell me, you young children of the multiverse, call by such names as 'The Milky Way,' or by such names as 'dark stars,' or 'dead stars' or 'nebulæ' or 'galaxies' or 'planets' or 'satellites of planets'—yes, what I have come to tell you is that all of us stars have decided between ourselves and without advice, and my old friend Mathonwy will bear me out here, from any god or any spirit or any creator or any life-force, or any life-energy, yes, purely and solely, I tell you, by our own will, our own desire, our own wish, our own conclusion, our own resolute and fixed determination, to bring to an end the whole business of celestial existence. We, the stars, have decided that all this praise of life which we have heard rising up from our own flesh and blood and from our own bowels is a wicked, cunning, crafty, treacherous, tricky, abominable *lie*! We have decided that this praise of Life is an outrage and an insult to all living things; and we stars know well enough of course that the minerals of which we are made, quite as much as the beasts, birds, reptiles, and fishes that we bring forth in air, water, earth, and perhaps even in fire, have all of them conscious nerves that are capable of suffering as well as conscious souls that are subject not only to unhappy moods but to misery and despair. We stars have therefore been holding a multi-cosmic conference for several million years, and our discussions at this conference have been lately growing more and more lively and intense. Indeed I think I may say we have reached a serious climax, the result of which looks very like a definite decision to end the whole thing, yes! the whole astronomical business, by a universal cosmogonic suicide. And now I must tell you that your approach to the general arena, or *agora*, as the old Greeks would say, of the region of our discussion, carried up as you have been by this fragment of your old green earth, has had a serious effect upon us stars. I greatly doubt whether my old acquaintance, Mathonwy, the father of the god Math who created Blodeuwedd out of flowers, realizes what the appearance of this flying landscape of yours means to us. We know, we stars of heaven, only too well what this little green landscape is. It is a planetary satellite that has rejected our stellar assembly's verdict in favour of universal suicide. I do not hesitate to reveal to you four earthlings, nor do I blush to reveal it in the presence of my old friend Mathonwy, the god of ancient Britain, that we have already put to death and dissolved, as we well know how to do, into complete and final extinction, all the other silly little life-maniacs who have behaved like this scrap of 'old mother earth,' as you love to call her, is behaving now. This little flying landscape of green grass must have realized by means of those psychic currents that pass through all forms of life what you two were thinking under your ailanthus tree in that great city. I do not quite know how far my old friend Mathonwy is following me in what I am telling you now, but I hope he is."

Here the star paused; and his great wheel of coloured lights made a slanting move, or tilt as you might put it, in the direction of Mathonwy. This pertinaciously pompous as he was also the obstinately propitiatory begetter of a whole pantheon of prehistoric divinities moved, I noticed, a little further off when those lights approached him. But Aldebaran now began a sardonic attack upon the green landscape under our feet.

"You must have said to yourself, you little scum of worm's meat and fading weeds: 'If I carry this loving couple sky high shall I not live by sucking the paps of their love? Shall I not live forever by loving those who will love each other forever? Shall I not make sport of these death-desiring stars by hugging to my heart these loving lovers?'" Thus did Aldebaran denounce our flying field.

It was probably my imagination but I certainly did think I felt the ground under my feet stir a little beneath this ferocious rebuke; and it struck me that Mathonwy himself floated still further away from us as if anxious to make it plain to Aldebaran that he dissociated himself from this life-worshipping vessel of grass and mud. But then to the obvious astonishment of the great glittering wheel, that was so to say, the outward intention of the inmost soul of this majestic star there appeared a new personality. Org and Asm and Rhitha and myself were astounded, and so most certainly was Mathonwy, who positively slid backwards through the air, as if his porcelain pedestal had possessed a pair of skates.

This newcomer was indeed a startling apparition. His figure was formed of some extremely malleable material that had been moulded into shape with exquisite precision and was now as hard as the hardest granite. Some accident had knocked off his head, but had not deprived him of it, for it hung at his side suspended by a delicate cord of living fibre through which the vital stream of nerves and blood and sensitized consciousness evidently still ran. This was made evident by the fact that it was through the lips of this suspended head that the newcomer addressed us all.

"There is no need," said the head, flickering its eyelids a little, but not giving any of us the sense that it was especially speaking to him or to her, far less to the brilliant wheel of Aldebaran's tremendous personality; "O no, no need at all for anybody here to ask who I am or why I have come. Each of you, including my lord Aldebaran, has only to look into the depths of himself and he will find the thing which you all, life-haters and life-lovers alike, have forgotten. What you have forgotten is the Way. Life has its work to do, and death ensues as if the common character of each were a thing ordered. You people consider that death has its cause, but that life has no cause. But is it really so? Heaven has its places and spaces that can be calculated. The divisions of the earth also can be assigned by men. But how shall we search for and find out the conditions of the Great Mystery? The Penumbræ once asked the Shadow: 'You were looking down and now you are looking up. Formerly you were walking and now you have stopped. How is all this?' "

It was then that one of the coloured lights in the wheel of the great star spoke and asked a question.

"My question is this," said the coloured light, "and I beg you to answer it plainly and simply: What sword is that which I see hidden in the folds of your dress?"

And the new-comer answered without a moment's hesitation: "It is the Sword of Heaven . . . it is regulated by the five elements . . . its unsheathing is like that of the Yin and the Yang. It is held fast in the spring and summer: it is put in action in the autumn and winter. When it is thrust forward there is nothing in front of it; when lifted up there is nothing above it; when laid down there is nothing below it; when wheeled round there is nothing left on any side of it: above, it cleaves the floating clouds, and below it penetrates to every division of the earth. This is the sword of the Son of Heaven."

Then did the great star of Aldebaran lift up his voice. "Who are you," he enquired, "who thus knows and understands the mystery of the Sword of Heaven?"

The voice of the great star was so authoritative that the small terra-cotta image became so anxious to satisfy him that he began with a pathetic stammer: "Kwa . . . Kwa . . . Kwa . . . Kwa . . . Kwa . . . Kwangtze is what they call me at home in China: but my enemies call me the stupid perverter of Laotze, because they contend that my interpretation of the *Tao* or the *Way* is a distortion of the writings of Laotze; when, on the contrary, they are the natural development of Laotze's teaching."

It was at this point that Mathonwy, who had been drawn (at least that is what I told myself) a little nearer by his aboriginal curiosity, could not resist uttering the stupid words: "Is this 'Tao' then, like me, a god who has been lost and found?"

At this question Kwangtze moved quite close up to this porcelain-pedestal'd one, who was pontificating around us like an imposing but evasive moth, and, when he could have touched him if he had wanted to do so, he replied:

"No, grandfather of the ancientest of Great Britons, I cannot say that I find any resemblance in you to the Tao. When my friend Po-Yu was in his sixtieth year his views became changed. He had never done anything but consider the views which he held to be absolutely right. But now he has come to condemn them as wrong. But Po-Yu does not realize at all that what he now calls right is what for fifty-nine years he has been calling wrong. All things have the life which we know. But we do not see its root. They have their goings forth but we do not know the door by which they depart. Ah! Ah! There is no escaping this. So it is! So it is!"

Something about the tone of Kwangtze and something about everything he said annoyed my friend Org to a point of fury. At last this multi-formed creature with something of the gorilla, something of the ox, something of the walrus, something of the hippopotamus, something of the seal, something of the camel, and a lot of the tortoise in him, burst out, "What do you think you are doing, you Chinese idol, talking to us in this respectful strain? My mate Asm here, and myself whose name is Org, have decided to follow this great scholar, Doctor Gor, and his lady-love Rhitha, in their wise determination to bring to an end the whole wretched crowd of living creatures who have been engendered or have been spawned, however you like to put it, upon the planets and their satellites, creatures who have been nurtured and matured by the heat of that radiant and royal star, our glorious Sun. Furthermore, you dribbling dotard of a heathen Chinese, it is my duty to inform you that this resplendent star Aldebaran, by the light of whose multi-coloured lanterns we are now sailing through the seventh-thousand Heaven, has just told us that at the great conference of all the stars in the sky the stars themselves have decided upon a universal suicide, and by this means, upon leaving Space as clean and healthy and bare and empty as it was in the old great times, when there was nothing there and when there was not anything anywhere."

"But, but, but, but, O superior man Org," protested Kwangtze, "have the sublime stars fully realized all the hidden implications in their momentous decision?"

At this point the shrill high-pitched voice of Asm piped up: "I am only a female, Professor Kwangtze, so forgive me if I speak crudely and bluntly! I don't know what you mean by the word 'implications,' but I know very well how nice it is when a house is entirely clean, and when there are no longer any bugs or fleas or lice or moths or beetles or rats or mice on the floor or in the cupboard!"

With my usual interest in every aspect of a situation that had any chance of ending in a general shindy, I had been keeping my eye on our pedestal'd deity, for whom Snowdon must have been a sort of Mount Olympus, and now when I saw him about to speak, I put my hand on Rhitha's arm, fearful lest she would have backed up Asm's words by referring to dust and ashes, or even to the webs of spiders.

"The most serious of the 'implications' referred to by our authority on the 'yin' and the 'yang' and on the true nature of the 'Tao,' is surely, or am I wholly lacking in metaphysical logic," so Mathonwy began, "the unavoidable deduction that since all of us will then be reduced to non-entity and non-existence, and since the whole cosmos will be nothing but empty space, or what we Ancient Britons used to call 'Diddym,' or the ultimate Void, things will have returned to their original condition before the creation of the World. No! I must not say 'things will have returned,' for there will be no 'things' there! The only word I can use is our old Welsh word 'Diddym,' *the Void.* All that is anything will then be nothing. But if this be so, O master of learning who hast come to us from the Celestial Empire, does it not prove that the god-like experiment of creating a world in space full of revolving masses of matter, possessed of the power of producing life from the four elements, has been a complete failure? For to make such a stupendous creation of so much from nothing at all into a success would surely, O Superior One from Pekin, have implied everlastingness in the created? And do not therefore the two voices to which we have listened—first the voice of the lives evolved from the stars and second the voice of the stars themselves, both of them advocating suicide—condemn all this servile, obsequious, cringing, sucking-up to, and all this lick-spittle polyglottic reverence for, the creation of the World, on the simple ground that it itself wants to perish?"

After this commentary upon the cosmogonic situation from the father of that powerful magician Math—who was the uncle of Gwydion the son of Don, and also the uncle of Arianrod, the mother of Llew Llaw Gyffes, for whom Math made a wife out of the blossoms of the meadow-sweet, the blossoms of the broom, and the blossoms of the oak and called her Blodeuwedd—there was a deep silence beneath the gleaming lights of Aldebaran. But lo and behold! another visitor from out of Space now appeared! And before the bewildered gaze of our two girls, who had instinctively once more seized each other's hands, and before us all who followed their gaze, appeared the palpable shape of Gautama Buddha! Yes! clear to the sight of every one of us was that familiar throne, that familiar lotus-leaf calm, and that to us unfamiliar trance of some inscrutable merging of the human in the divine!

Calmly for a space that image regarded us; and then at length, "I have been persuaded to leave Nirvana," were the words that floated out into the air from that enthroned figure; though, closely as I scrutinized this prophet of the pure intellect, I could not see his lips moving, "in order to ask both the star Aldebaran and this Earth-landscape which so boldly refuses to commit suicide, whether ordered to do so by an assembly of stars or by an assembly of the most articulate creatures projected by the planets of these stars, I have come, I say, to ask them both if there isn't a possible *third course* that could be taken, which were neither suicide nor defiance of the will to commit suicide?"

It was at this moment, while everybody waited for some answer to the Buddha's calm but authoritative words, that my Rhitha suddenly jumped up from the grass and rushed to the side of Kwangtze, and lifting up his head from the end of his jangled, jerked, jowled, jiggered, jockeyed, jungled, jumbled, joggled, jabboranded neck, she held it gently against her own body, not so much like a mother as like a sympathetic sister, and held it in such a position that he could see through the air the Buddha upon his throne floating quite close to Mathonwy upon his pedestal.

The Buddha missed nothing of what Rhitha had done. "Let his head rest now, little lady," he said. "I will see to it that there shall be a cushion beneath it."

Rhitha obediently but extremely slowly and cautiously released the head of Kwangtze, which, sure enough, did promptly relax upon a willowy, billowy, pillowy cloud, of a beautiful dark-blue tint such as the waves of the sea sometimes wear at the close of twilight.

"How did it happen, O last of all the Superior Ones, whom I expected to meet in these empty regions, that your neck was pulled out to such a pitiful length?"

"It was done, O Kohinoor of wisdom, by a couple of impetuous lovers, one from the furthest possible distance from the ocean in his island midlands, and the other from the furthest possible distance from the ocean in her continental midlands; the one from the Old World and the other from the New World, but each of them entirely devoid of that quality which only sailors possess."

"And what quality may that be, O friend of Laotze and critic of Confucius?"

"Keeping one's head!" replied Kwangtze with a chuckle; "and may I," he added, "be permitted to keep this divine cushion when you, its beatific bestower, return to Nirvana across the Ganges?"

It was clear to me, as I watched carefully the features of the enthroned Buddha, that among innumerable qualities with which Brahma or Para-Brahma had endowed him there was not the faintest tinge of the quality of humour. Not a flicker of the faintest smile at this sally of the demi-decapitated Kwangtze crossed that sublime countenance. But my attention was soon drawn away from both Kwangtze's foolery and Gautama's gravity by the resonant voice of Aldebaran enquiring with lucid directness just what was this *third path* that might lead us out of this great cosmic dilemma. The answer from that lotus-surrounded seat of judgment evidently struck both our ladies as the right and just one, for they clasped hands just as they had done at the beginning of our adventure, and waved their free arms in exultant agreement.

"Let all who wish to perish perish," was the Buddha's judicial decision, "and let all who wish to live live!"

And then I realized that the masculine minds of Org and myself did not agree with this. I mean that the sort of free chaos or general anarchy of individual choice suggested by the Buddha's final words—yes! and the lotus throne *had* vanished after this judicial utterance and the visitor from Nirvana had returned whence he came—was more in harmony with a woman's feelings than with a man's. A man feels a longing to organize and execute elaborate strategy and exhaustive tactics, whereas a woman takes each situation on its own ground.

During the very act of exchanging this thought between ourselves—and after all, though I am an egoistic orator-actor and Org is a mythological and multiple mixture of fish, bird, beast and reptile, we had come to understand each other pretty well—our attention was distracted by a totally unexpected flash of lightning and roll of thunder and out of the centre of a dark cloud that came sailing by over our heads we heard going on the most extraordinary argument that I've ever heard in all my whole life!

I hadn't seen any natural cloud for a long time; for the grey rim of the circular landscape, which was now carrying us into space, might have been smoke or mist or water, and around us on all sides now was nothing but dusky, though not pitch-black, empty air: and the sight of this natural cloud, just the sort of cloud that I have seen so often in early afternoons in Blaenau, and a sister-cloud to so many other familiar ones such as I used to see when I went to Llandderfel in my courting days to visit Rhitha. And yet, here was this ordinary, natural cloud, sailing along, only about a hundred yards above our heads and out of it was proceeding such a colloquy as neither Rhitha nor I, nor Org or Asm, had ever dreamed of hearing, and certainly were never likely to hear again.

"If you want me to sleep with you tonight," was what the most beautiful feminine voice it is possible for me to imagine was now saying, "you must interfere at once in this dastardly business and prevent these mad stars and these mad people from playing this preposterous game with a life-force they have neither created nor can understand."

"You talk too loud and you talk too quick, Hera, my darling bedfellow. It is in order to have this question fully threshed out that I have brought you all with me here, where we can get some inkling of what these stars and these mortal earth-creatures are up to. I confess their intentions and purposes strike me so far, from what we have been listening to, as if they had completely lost what little reason they may originally have possessed."

"Would it not be a good thing," another female voice broke in, a voice that had a certain masculine resonance mixed with its mellow feminine sagacity, "if I were to put on my armour and take my spear and shield and go down there and confront them all?"

"What I want to know," a man's voice began in so hoarse and husky a manner that it was clear the speaker was extremely old: "is whether this ground is a portion of the bosom of Mother Gaia, and, if it is, I want to know where the rest of her is?"

At this there was clearly audible among these newcomers a rumble like thunder, and I could see that Aldebaran, with his coloured lights and with that curious effect of a wheel which emanated from him, was suddenly sliding away from us in a direction opposite to the one from which this Olympian cloud had descended.

"Are you still, O my crazy begetter," said a voice that

I knew by instinct to be the voice of Zeus himself, "so devoted to your old Mother the Earth that you can't get it into your head that with us immortals every portion of our bodies is——"

It was clear at this point that an older, wider, fainter, weirder, remoter, much more mysterious voice intervened, a voice much less allied to the feelings of us mortals or even to the feelings of a radiant star like Aldebaran; and at the sound of *this* voice it was evident to me that the ground under my feet shivered a little, as if with the hearing of it some ancient wrong came back, some appalling outrage done to her—long before Mathonwy in Britain, or Kwangtze in China, or Gautama Buddha in India, had been raised by Fate, or by Destiny, or by Chance, or perhaps simply by Necessity, to their present thrones—had given her whole nature a shock and all her flesh a hurt and an outrage so great that its effect could never pass away.

"It was thou thyself, O Kronos," responded Ouranos, "that with the jagged flint she gave thee didst scatter wide upon the waters the live seed of thy own fathers loins!"

"Have you forgotten," retorted Kronos, "how your vile lust-work upon the tender flesh of my mother the Earth forced her to give birth to monsters, yes! to creatures who fouled her delicate body with a hideous brutality only suited to Tartaros and Erebos? Have you forgotten this?"

It was then—while it seemed to me that all of us who were present, whether mortal or immortal, whether male or female, waited with a curiously desperate interest the issue of this debate, as if something far more serious than victory in argument hung upon it, yes! as if something of cosmic importance were at stake—that my sweet Rhitha, white and trembling, suddenly clung to my neck and whispered in my ear: "Gor, darling Gor, I've seen that awful face! And, do you know, it is . . . it is the same appalling fiend I saw nibbling at the rim of the moon!"

"Hush, hush, my sweet!" I whispered back to her, "we mustn't disturb this honourable company with our mad individual visions of fear and terror! Besides, any of these powerful beings could drive that greedy devil back into his native hell!"

"But he's whispering to me, Gor darling! O, I'm so frightened of him!"

"He can't hurt you here, my sweet!" I whispered. "Do for heaven's sake be careful! I don't want them to hear you!"

But my own curiosity broke out just then and I begged Rhitha to ask him what his name was. Such trust in me did my darling have that she obeyed me at once with some soundless question in the depths of her heart which the devil up there, invisible to the rest of us, could hear, and not only could hear, but was impelled to answer.

"O Gor, Gor," Rhitha murmured, while the sharp little nail of the longest finger with which she clung to my neck caused me considerable discomfort—indeed I fancied I felt little drops of blood from it running down under my vest. "He says," she explained to me, "that his name is Moloch; and that he is the god of the people who lived in Palestine before the Israelites came there, and that he hates the Jews more bitterly than any of us Christians hate them. O Gor darling"—and here her voice shivered till it was scarcely audible; for it was clear that this appalling fiend whose name was Moloch had terrified my girl into a wild panic—"O Gor! Darling Gor! Do you know what he says? He says that he will have me sacrificed on his——"

She was interrupted by the sudden appearance at our side of the kindest, gentlest, most comforting being I have ever seen in my whole life. She was a goddess—I was absolutely sure of *that*, but it was impossible not to be so reassured by her presence that you didn't care whether she was a mortal or an immortal; she was just a lady, a woman, a female, and one under whose protection you felt you were safe forever. This being took my Rhitha's ice-cold forehead in her two hands, and when she had kissed it and released it, she whispered to us both: "Don't you be afraid of Moloch. I know him and all his little games. He's after my daughter up there now! But I'll make them all follow me—and maybe our father Zeus with a well-aimed thunderbolt will do for that wretch forever! I'll beg him to! But I must get them all there to rescue Aphrodite anyway! So don't you worry, either of you!"

In a moment she was off and had entered that Olympian cloud, and *that* also in a moment was off, and Rhitha and I could see it growing smaller and smaller and smaller, till it finally disappeared. And I now felt a pressing need to change my attitude to what was happening. Yes, I must give up this pose of reverential expectation and adopt a quite different tone. I had no sooner decided this when an event occurred of a nature so startling as to sweep into the limbo of forgotten things all that I expected or was pretending to expect.

The whole ground upon which we stood, with its circular horizon of what might have been either grey mist or grey water, began to heave and shake. Evidently, judging from the domestic altercation we had just heard, between the voice of Kronos and the voice of Ouranos, this living fragment of the sacred flesh of Gaia, the ancient Earth, was anxious to make it clear to the present company of living consciousnesses gathered about her that she definitely refused to join this suicidal pact of the existing inhabitants, whether human, subhuman, or superhuman, whether animal, vegetable, or mineral, of this universe, or this multiverse, or this cosmos or this Congeries of Cosmoi, and had decided to shake them all off, to reject and falsify their unworthy hatred of life because life brought suffering, and to go on living at all cost and in spite of all, until, if at last she was forced to die, she would die fighting for life! I looked at Rhitha and took her hand; and we called upon Org and Asm to come close to us, which they unhesitatingly did; and the graceful Asm took Rhitha's free hand, and the grotesquely-shaped Org allowed me to clutch with my five human fingers one of his semi-marine, semi-river-swamp tusks. So there we four were, holding fast together in a line of self-defence. But it must be admitted that we were by no means certain as to which side we were on; since we sympathized so utterly with the idea that to live was *not enough compensation* for the sufferings and miseries of life, but at the same time we were, all four of us, without question so linked with, so involved with, so concerned with, so entwined with, so grounded on and founded on, our mother the earth that it was impossible for us, whether called upon to do so by all the angels of heaven or by all the devils of hell, to separate ourselves from her.

But something about the resolution and independence

of this fragment of our old earth, combined with this heaving and rocking of everything beneath our feet, including green grass and grass-mould and gravel and rock-sand and stones of basalt and bits of granite, had a remarkable effect upon all the visitors who had recently descended or ascended, like celestial vultures, upon our privacy. The first to go was Kwangtze, who although considerably absorbed, as the folds of his Chinese garments swirled about him like disordered sails on a drifting ship, with the one important task of keeping his head on his shoulders, did not fail to utter from that same head a Taoistic goodbye.

"Perfect enjoyment," he bade us all remember, "is to be without enjoyment; the highest praise is to be without praise. Heaven does nothing and thence comes its serenity. Earth does nothing and thence comes its rest. By the union of these two inactivities all things are produced. How vast and imperceptible is the process! Heaven and Earth do nothing, and yet there is nothing that they do not do!"

Certainly, when Kwangtze was gone, either independently of the Tao he had been teaching us or under its patient influence, Nothingness spread her indescribable wings and floated over our heads like a vast moth. And then I realized that Mathonwy also was leaving us forever, for down upon us from his departing pedestal was wafted the old Welsh word "Diddym," meaning "The Ultimate Void." And finally, at the very last, bequeathing to all four of us the weird sensation of being more than just absolutely alone, the great star Aldebaran, with all his coloured lights turning and burning in their revolving wheel about him, shot out of sight.

Led by an instinct that must have been entirely different in each of us four, we fell side by side on our knees: that is to say we three human-shaped earthlings knelt, while Org lowered first a jungle-hairy, desert-bony, prairie-skinny knee and then a sea-ribbed, ocean-bladdered, swamp-bulbous knee, and while we three gazed inevitably upwards, to the emptiness above, Org with his sub-oceanic eye-balls protruding out of his head stared straight in front of him towards the horizon.

Thus we all four remained; and my own impression is that every single one of us, not excluding our dear grotesque Org, enjoyed, during those few moments, the most intense realization of the Self and Not-Self—I mean of the self that feels itself to be itself, and of the outward objects at which that inner self looks out and which include that inner self's own body and that inner self's own bodily senses, by means of which that inner self grasps the nature of the Not-Self, which surrounds it, as it surrounds all of us, on every side.

I know I am trying to describe the feelings of each of us four at that moment in a heavy ponderous pedantic manner, but that has been the fault of my family for many generations. The truth is we Blaenau people—for our very name means "further on"—have an instinctive tendency to what you might call the *dramatics of metaphysics*, in other words a taste for dramatizing all the "acts" and "scenes" of philosophical speculation, just as if the ultimate categories of Time and Space themselves were only really interesting and exciting as the background to the stage-set of the drama of our individual life. We have only to glance at the sympathetic treatment of the people of Wales, whether as great princes like

Glendower, or as plain men like Fluellen in the plays, to see what a terrific influence on Shakespeare the Welsh attitude to life exercized, just as it did on Milton; and in both these cases the influence was on identical lines if you cut out the comic touch along with its Welsh retort—"if you can mock a leek, you can eat a leek!" In other words it encouraged the two greatest of the world's poets, only rivalled by Homer and by Dante and by Goethe, to turn our philosophical attitude to the ultimate mystery of existence into emotional and dramatic acts and scenes of a personal play.

All the world's a stage
And all the men and women merely players.

Thus, as I tried later to analyse the strange feelings that we four—two males and two females—experienced at that moment in our lives, although it is, I fancy, pretty certain that nobody really can speak for anybody but himself, what struck me most powerfully was the queer fact that, though we had round us so few of the objects with which we generally satisfy our longing for Nature's wonders, our emotional response to the vast Not-Self was not lessened but increased. I may be speaking only for myself, but I think not. We were all so utterly surrounded by infinite endlessness that it seems to me our emotions must have been, if not identical, at least very similar. Anyhow we were all reduced to an awed silence; and one thing at least is certain, namely that the feelings which passed through us have never been expressed in the world before, because they have never been felt in the world before.

As the first shock wore off, or perhaps it would be more appropriate to say toned down, we all four automatically crouched down on the grass and "took," as we say, "stock" of our extraordinary situation.

It was neither daylight where we found ourselves now, nor was it what we all four had come to call twilight. Of the two twilights familiar to us, the morning twilight and the evening twilight, what we were now experiencing was more like the morning one in its general psychic effect on our nerves, for it brought with it complete uncertainty as to what was going to happen next; whereas with the evening twilight there are always hints and tokens and signs, outside us as well as inside us, of the approach of all that the word sleep suggests to tired mortals.

There were no clouds. There was no mist. There were no heavenly bodies to be recognised by the quality of their starry lights, or by their zodiacal arrangements like some cosmic wizard's sorcery-map of celestial predictions hung up for all his pawns and puppets to see. There was simply nothing, where we four were crouching in a group, from the horizon to the zenith; nothing north, nothing south, nothing east, nothing west. It certainly was a queer sensation to feel that if we could fly to any single point in that vast aerial dome above our heads, and if we were able to mount up from that particular point—up and out, out and up, whether with our grassy landscape or without our grassy landscape—we could ascend for ever and still find nothing.

"Come, my friends," I said at last, "let's decide what we'd better do now."

The idea of deciding what to do in an emptiness as complete as this certainly struck a rather comical note.

The phrase "decide what to do" is so pathetically sensible that my question was as if a saint in heaven had enquired where they kept their soap. I did not miss the fact that, as soon as I had spoken, our two young ladies' hands met in an instinctive self-protective gesture. They must have felt, though my darling Rhitha really knew me too well to indulge long in such feelings, that after all my heroic talk about a universal suicide in the face of the cruel sufferings of life, I might start suggesting to Org that, before finishing ourselves off, it might be well to begin with the sacrifice of our frailer companions. At any rate with a vague idea of lessening the solemnity of the desperate silence we had all fallen into, I abruptly asked a question which I had longed to ask ever since Rhitha and I first encountered this queer pair.

"By the way, Org, forgive me if it's a rude question, but where and when did you and Asm first meet?"

"No difficulty about answering him on that point, is there, old girl?" replied Org, with what might have been called a chuckle, but which really was a multiple sound containing that indescribable noise that certain fish make when they receive a deadly blow, and also containing a distorted hee-haw with something in it of a groan of utter weariness, and also something in it of a gulp of pure amusement, such as an overloaded donkey, observing a baby greedily sucking a carrot, might make.

Seeing that his lovely little slender lady gave him a sympathetic smile, Org went on: "I was the product, my friend, if you really want to know"—and as I heard him I had an odd feeling as if we were in a church or temple, but not a temple to the Divinity announced by Jesus, but to a god altogether unknown to the human race and worshipped only by four-legged animals—"the product," Org continued, "of one of the experiments of these vivisectionists. Whether they did it in London, or in New York or in Paris or in some university outside these big cities, I cannot say. As you two have discovered for yourselves the cruelties deliberately indulged in, under the excuse of benefiting the human race, but in reality solely to satisfy the twin lusts of these fiendish men—a lust for cruelty for its own sake and a lust for knowledge for its own sake, two appalling lusts both inhuman and dehumanizing, and both of them as un-christian as the most horrible barbarities of the ancient Chinese, and when combined together, as they are with these vivisectionists, culminating in cruelties such as would make Tiberius and Caligula and Nero, and even Gilles de Retz himself, as these devils thirst for new victims in the diverse hells of their own hearts, shiver with envy!"

If my words about "deciding what to do" had sounded queer in our present situation, this philosophical and historical discourse from a creature as grotesque-looking as Org struck us all as absolutely fantastic. But Org went on, as sublimely unconscious, as we all are, when beside ourselves with indignation, of any incongruity:

"Every living thing trembles with terror at the presence of any single one of these abominable men, men who deliberately and daily practise cruelties that would make a sworn tormentor from the Spanish Inquisition gasp. Well, I was created by these vivisectionists in a manner I need not harrow your feelings by describing. But they made the mistake of not allowing for the development of my intelligence. Of course what they chiefly enjoy is practising upon response-nerves; but they are all so obsessed by this *double-lust*, the lust to cause pain and the lust to get knowledge, that, like other cruelty-drunk beings, they so kill their normal human feeling that, unless their unspeakable practices become illegal, the whole human race may, when a few more centuries have passed, be entirely ruled by these demons *of Knowledge through Cruelty*.

"Well, as I was saying, the one thing they forgot, and you can bet it *would* be the thing in their damnable inhumanity that they'd naturally forget, was the growth, under their little games, of my intelligence. Well, the result of this was that I escaped. And what then? Why then, quite naturally, I made for the sea; and by some rapid swimming, and also by the splendid device of clinging to whatever was available in the sterns of the fastest vessels I encountered, I managed to approach an island from which voices of the far-off past called out to me and promised to find me a companion; and it was here that I met Asm who had done exactly what I had done—that is to say, escaped. The people who were cruel to her after her parents in Llandderfel were dead were relatives living in an island in the north of Britain—the isle in fact that the ancient Romans used to call 'Ultima Thule,' though today it has another name, a name which Asm wants to forget. She escaped from it by joining some group of adventurers; and it was among the mounds of the lost gods of Easter Island that we met, and it was among the mounds of the lost gods that we 'plighted our troth,' as Asm has taught me to call it. She was never frightened of me or horrified at me. From the first she was the same Asm that she is today——"

"But how on earth," I began, and then remembering

that, wherever we were on this fragment of Mother Gaia, we could hardly be said to be "on earth," "how," I went on, "did you two learn to fly through the air?"

"O *that* little trick is due to Asm's credit entirely," the queer monster hurriedly replied: "She had been to an electricity school and being far more intelligent than any other pupil or indeed than any teacher there and being as original in her ideas as I am in mine, and being also——"

Here the lovely Asm jumped up, put her hand on the monster's mouth, gave his protuberant snout a touch with her upper lip, and sat down again.

"Yes, hers entirely," Org continued. "Under my scales here," and he scraped the back of one of his fins with the tip of one of his hooves, "I've got a neat little ball of electrified feathers; and Asm has got a similar one in that leather purse in her belt, and we were voyaging fast through the air to the coast of Scotland, when, with a rush of meteor-fire and a spurt of lights in the shape of a wheel, the star Aldebaran overtook us and swept us along in its resplendent trail."

"Have you and Asm," I enquired, "changed your opinion as to the desirability of all the creatures of our old planet Earth sacrificing themselves in one supreme act of self-immolation, or, to put it more bluntly, of suicide, or have you reverted, after hearing the words of the mother of Aphrodite, to the old-fashioned notion held by our parents that self-murder is a wicked and blasphemous act?"

There was a considerable pause among us four persons after this speech from me. But Org answered at last:

"Yes," he said, "I veritably believe there *has* been a

change in my opinion on this important point; but I don't think it was under the influence of the mother of Venus-Aphrodite, nor of the many-coloured wheel of the star that swept us down here, that this change occurred. I really do believe, though you may laugh at me for saying so, that my present inclination to reject this self-destructive pact is the result of several years of silent and secret cogitations while growing up to become what I am under the hands of these criminally cruel vivisectors. You see, these wicked and abominable men, obsessed by their mania for knowledge at any price, have completely distorted all natural human pity, all natural human consideration, all natural human feeling; so that what they have really done in all these probings and proddings into the most sensitive nerves they could find was simply to kill the thing in themselves which common humanity has come to call our Conscience. This being dead, they now can go steadily forward with their astounding collection of careful data about the psychological, pathological, neuropathic reactions to pain and discomfort, displayed by every organism in the world that Nature has endowed with sensitivity to suffering. And this interminable portfolio of writhings and squirmings, this well-indexed extravaganza of paroxyms of terror, this accumulative register of what man can do to his fellow animals, is being kept purely for knowledge, yes! for knowledge for its own sake. 'Now,' says the scripture, 'abideth faith, hope and charity,' but the vivisectionists say: 'far greater than any of these is knowledge.' And consider also, my dear friends," and as Org went on I was touched to see the worship in Asm's eyes as she regarded him, "what a poor, thin, hollow, echoing cavern of misery and of despair, knowledge would be if it were all we had! There would we *stand*, there would we *sit*, there would we *lie* with sensitive bodies, minds, adventurous imaginations, all withered up in this accumulation of vivisectional details about experiments on living nerves, without the faintest chance of exerting what is the most godlike of all powers, namely the power of creation! For how, I ask you, my kind friends, how in the name of the supreme Demon, could any creature who knew everything that could be known, who possessed in fact all the knowledge that these insane scientists, by means of their incalculable cruelties, are seeking to get, how could such a creature be moved by any exciting desire or emotion as he huddled down in this transparent vision of all knowledge? The only way it could be made tolerable—don't you agree with me, Gor? don't you agree with me, Rhitha? —would be if by some lucky chance there were to appear some little tiny knot of contrariety in the infinite sameness of this glassy, horny, horizonless, purposeless, monotonous, and most horribly comprehensible cosmos, just one tiny little speck or blob or atom of inexplicable mystery! But there isn't one jot or tittle of such a thing! Science understands all. What it can never understand are the feelings, the moods, the fancies, the thoughts, the caprices, the manias, the whimsies, the emotions of one single living creature! And it is this that so infuriates these inquisitors of vivisection, as they go on pinching and probing and poking and pricking and persecuting and pillorying the nerve-centres and nerve-channels of every creature they can catch in order to collect in their note-books, every conceivable twinge of pain and shrinking from pain."

So exhausted was our poor multi-membered Org by this long swim in the waves of oratory, that he now sank down on the green grass with a sigh like that of an enormous octopus, under a mile of salt water.

It was at this point in our extraordinary adventure that I became conscious of two significant things. The first of these things was that our ladies had once more joined hands. And the second was that the field of green grass on which we were travelling through space was stirring and heaving again in its own body.

I moved up closer to Rhitha, for we were all aware of a premonition of the coming of some event completely different in its nature from anything that had so far happened.

And as I moved to Rhitha's side, for the three of us who were bipeds were now on our feet, Org, our terraqueous monster—whose appearance suggested that his vivisecting creators had tried to intermingle a walrus with a hippopotamus and to bestow on the issue of this mixture the fins of a shark and the feathers of a wild-goose—moved simultaneously to Asm's side, so that we were now just as we had been when we saw that sticky and slimy python Eternity perish by the horrible greed with which it devoured Time. But all around us now was nothing but hollow, empty, purposeless, meaningless space, extending without limit in every direction, and you can believe, if anything in my tale remains credible to you, how ridiculous to us four living beings—as we felt all around us the tasteless, colourless, impalpable, viewless, scentless, indefinable presence of boundless space—would have been the idea that the universe had some thinkable limit and did not stretch out forever in all directions, of the still more ridiculous idea that it had a definite beginning or when the hour comes will have a definite end.

And then—yes, even as we waited in a weird sort of coma, or trance, or enchanted suspension of all normal thought—we distinctly saw in the air above us the enormous superhuman features of two colossal countenances, one on the left and one on the right, evidently belonging to a couple of supernatural beings who were clearly disputing between themselves upon some abysmal topic.

I knew without being told, for she pressed my fingers with a convulsive clutch, that Rhitha was reminded of the vulture face of her enemy Moloch as she gazed at the colossal countenance on the left, but being something of a virtuoso in demons I knew well that this one was far more formidable. In any case we all four listened spellbound and enthralled by what we were hearing, not to speak of what we were seeing, when one or the other of us dared to look at one or the other of those two faces.

"Have you changed your opinion, Satan?" said the right-hand face to the left-hand face, "about the Beginning of things?"

"You mean about the Beginning of the universe?" answered the left-hand face.

"That's what I mean," affirmed the right-hand one, "because, if you have, I should dearly love to hear what new idea you have got."

"As for yourself, Jehovah," queried Satan, "I suppose you still go on with your old illusion that you actually created this universe that has now entirely vanished, with the exception of that absurd scrap down there, of the wretched little planet called Earth upon which you pretend you created Adam and Eve as the ancestors of the human race, of whom some still worship you as their god

—although, as I have so often compelled you to admit, in those days you were not the god of any tribe of mortals except the Jews, who are now so oddly separated from all other races and so ridiculously hated by so many stupid and ignorant people? So you still think of yourself, do you, as the Creator of this universe whose miserable earthlings have recently destroyed themselves and whose 'nebulæ' and 'galaxies,' as they call them, of suns and stars have now imitated them and done themselves in too? If, as you boast, you really did create this beastly universe, that has now finished itself off except for that cheese-paring of a bowling-green down there and the disgusting little maggots that are crawling about on it, is, I ask you, this creation of creatures who find life so unpleasant that their only desire is to kill themselves, anything to boast of?"

Jehovah smiled.

"Shall I never be able to make you see, O stupidest and silliest of all possible Satans, that the only thing worth having, whether within or without the universe is consciousness? All matter is conscious, just as I am and just as you are, and all that it gives birth to is conscious also. All air is conscious with all that lives in it. All water is conscious in the same way with all its offspring, and so also is fire. You, Satan, are only yourself and only happy in yourself when you are hating and destroying. Of course there are a lot of things, and a lot of spirits and souls, that you *cannot* destroy; and for that very reason you hate them more than you hate the ones you *can* destroy. But I beg you to consider this problem a little closer. What, let me ask you, O great hater and destroyer, is enjoyment in life? What is it that prevents you, yes, you yourself, the great Demon of the universe, from ending your life, when you know very well that in the battle between you and me neither of us can ever win, and neither of us can destroy the other? Shall I tell you what prevents you with all your mania for killing from killing yourself? Nothing less than your worship of self-consciousness! Once dead, your consciousness of being alive would be gone, and as far as you were concerned, you not only would not be yourself any more, but you very well might *never have been at all*.

"Now it is a queer thing, my good Satan, if you will permit your ancient antagonist to use a syllable as unpleasing to your ears as 'good,' how tenacious most created creatures are of life, and yet how not only recklessly and desperately but even casually and carelessly they will throw away life for all sorts of fanciful purposes that are neither according to *my* will nor according to *your* will—for such purposes I mean that are neither creative nor destructive, but are simply playful. In fact what both of us, you as a breaker-down, and I as a builder-up according to our different natures, take seriously, these queer human creatures of the planet Earth take like a game. And now apparently this infection of play-acting—caught I daresay from these capricious and whimsical descendants of Adam with his Garden and of Noah with his Ark—has affected all the constellations and all the stars, so that they also are enjoying this pretty little silly dramatic game of killing themselves, and as far as I can see—and I believe I can see quite as far as you can if not further—most of them, and, in a minute or two, all of them, will have finished doing it, and you and I and these four wretched little entities on this scrap of flying greenery will be the only conscious selves left alive in Space."

Here the right-hand countenance of the two terrific faces that were now looking straight down upon us permitted itself to indulge in the most extraordinary smile I have ever seen in my whole mortal life. Nor was I lacking in the intelligence to notice another thing, though whether our dear monster Org had the wit to see it too I haven't the faintest idea. He certainly kept exchanging very significant glances with his partner Asm; so very likely he *had* seen it! What I saw was this; and I knew well by the pressure of her fingers that my Rhitha had caught it too. There had passed across the demonic countenance on the left a shiver of unquestionable panic! It didn't last, but it had undoubtedly shown itself. And I asked myself just what particular word from the lips of the face on the right had caused this spasm of fear? Or was it simply the indescribable depth of his companion's smile, a smile that certainly struck me as if it were the whole of space smiling, or rather—for I couldn't even *imagine* space *as a whole*, as if it were as much of space as I could grasp with my limited human mind—smiling at me, at my fumbling mind, at all four of us standing so pathetically on that grassy field, and finally, so it seemed to me, and it was this very likely that so scared the Devil, at the whole crazy situation? It was then that a voice from the face on the right spoke again.

"Have I, my only companion for millions of centuries, to repeat still once more for your forgetful ears the tale of our first meeting? Well! I have at least the excuse of those four little creatures on that shred of terrestrial greenery down there; for I can see, as no doubt you can also see, that they're listening to our colloquy with no small interest. And so with the excuse of their presence I'll go over the same old story again."

We four were indeed petrified with interest as Jehovah went on.

"It all began of course, as you very well know, with our mutual awakening from sleep in infinite space. And here's a very nice point, my dear Devil, that I may have forgotten to make in any of the million occasions when I've reviewed these things. Long after the composing of any of the primeval stories about how things began, in fact, in comparatively recent discussions as to how they began, the philosophers of the satellite of the sun, from which those four insects down there derive their existence, developed a trick of talking with pompous authority about what they called 'the Absolute.' With this ridiculous 'Absolute' of theirs they wanted to get the infantile conclusion established that there was a final Something that partook partly of the nature of consciousness and partly of the nature of matter, and that included everything that existed, that had ever existed, and that would ever exist. They brought forward this idea for the obvious reason that they were too proud, too vain, and too conceited to confess frankly and freely that the limited nature of their human intelligence debarred them from the comprehension of any ultimate aspect of existence except boundless space; and that all they can do, and all they will ever be able to do, is to fall back upon their consciousness of the unlimited, unending space in which they appear and into which they will dissolve when they disappear. Is it not clear at a glance to you, my dear Devil, as it is clear to me, that in the midst of this boundless space wherein we are now conversing it is nonsense to talk of 'the Absolute' in the sense of something that *is* all there is, and that *includes* all there is, and beyond which there is nothing at all, unless by this grandiose word is meant just simply and plainly empty space. In *that* sense both I, the Creator and Protector of whatever is in space, and you, the Destroyer and Corrupter of whatever is in space, will be in full agreement with each other when we say that such a vacant, hollow container, for me to fill at will and for you to spill at will, can hardly be called an Absolute, if by that tremendous word is meant some substantial reality that rests at the bottom of all possible worlds. And note this too, my dear Devil, with regard to this blessed word Absolute. Their less educated ones are naturally puzzled by this grand word; and so their cleverer ones derive a deliciously superior comfort and complacency and an almost lord-of-the-manor satisfaction from the idea that to enjoy the Absolute is a mystical privilege, if not a sensual privilege, confined to a very few philosophic minds. But what I particularly want you, my dear Devil, to realize is——"

But the Devil broke in here with a howl of boredom.

"I tell you, God," he yelled, "I shall scream this blasted space of yours into the parings of a pilgarlic pipistrel if you don't stop talking about Absolutes! You promised once to tell me the whole story of how you and I first came to know each other. You've given me so much to do with your bloody creations and your blasted redemptions that for millions of years I've not had a moment's rest; but since, except for these four wretched little entities, your conglomerated creation seems at this moment to have taken to its heels, leaving us idle for a bit, this might be a good moment for you to keep that promise."

"Well, old companion," God answered gently, "I am almost inclined to accede to your request, only we had better lower our voices and turn our faces away from those pathetic little creatures down there."

At this the Devil gave a hoarsely croaking chuckle.

"O how sweetly considerate you sound! Just as if you didn't know as well as I do that those insects are listening breathlessly to every word we speak. Really, for pure and simple humbug, God, you beat all the miserable little creatures for whose unhappy life you are responsible, and who are now showing what they think of you and your redemptive ability by committing suicide. However! I am not a humbug like you, and I do very much want to hear your story. So please tell it."

"Well," God began, in a quiet meditative tone, "I'll do my best. But I am better at creation than at describing creation. But it certainly was an extraordinary experience, that moment of waking slowly into the consciousness of being conscious—of being, that is to say, a self that had the power of saying to itself '*I am I.*'

"I sometimes long to startle some of the more obsequious of my adorers by forcing them to listen to an explanation, by a few insects and a few snails and a few newts and a few tadpoles and a few shrimps and a few sticklebacks, of what it feels like when you first say '*I am I*'! And then I'd like to make them listen to you and me talking about *our* first awareness of being alive! It would certainly amuse——"

But as God uttered the word "amuse," I didn't miss—nor did my Rhitha, as I could tell from the pressure of her fingers—the extremely interesting fact that there passed across the face of the Devil that same queer shudder of what I can only describe as panic-terror which had seized him when his everlasting antagonist smiled. Was any kind of humour then—that is to say the power of being amused by some word or event or accident or situation, the power in fact of appreciating the incorrigible, the ineradicable comedy of the whole bloody business of life—essentially godlike, and its opposite, the inability to see the funny or comic or ironic side of things, inherently devilish? No! no! no! Such a theory, if we accepted it in its entirety, would mean that all living creatures, save only men, women, and children, were on the side of the Devil, which is wholly unthinkable, in spite of the way some of us persist in talking about "cloven hooves" and "vipers' tongues" and "vultures' claws" and "sharks' teeth" and so forth! But my thoughts were now interrupted by the divine voice itself; for God had begun to relate to the Devil his first experience of being God.

"My first feeling, or thought, if you like, was not any sort of consciousness of a 'self' or of an 'ego' or of an 'I am I'; it was purely, simply, and solely an intense interest that grew steadily more and more intense, in what I was looking at with my two eyes. And do you know what I was looking at? *At you!* Yes, you were with me, and moreover you were doing exactly what I was doing, that is to say you were looking round, and you were, just as I was—and what could be more natural?—thrilled with interest at seeing me there! So that the truth is that just as *my* first awareness, or *my* first sensation, or *my* first experience, of being alive, was *my* interest in you, so your first was *your* interest in me. So there we were! But, after that initial recognition of each other, our two consciousnesses must have debouched and deviated, each upon its own separate track. As I watched you I was wondering in my own mind whether you were a portion of myself, whether in truth I was a double-being possessed not only of two outward appearances but also of two inward intelligences. Were we in fact, two separate minds that could tap each other's reservoirs of thought but yet at the source were really and truly one; two separate streams, no doubt, when once they started running, but streams that were flowing from the same primal fountain-head? It was a considerable surprise to me, Devil old friend, when I suddenly noticed that your attention had wandered from me to the infinite space that surrounded us and that you were searching every horizon of this vast emptiness around us to discover, so it occurred to me, if there had been any other double-natured beings like ourselves born at this moment for no reason out of nothing. But this sudden discovery of mine that our mental and emotional interests did not correspond, but that you were now scrutinizing with eager curiosity the hollow gulfs of empty space, whereas I was absorbed solely and exclusively with this immediate problem of our relation to each other, was not only a considerable shock to me, but was an important turning-point in my mental development.

"If we were not the same being, I asked myself, possessed, as I had hitherto imagined, of two heads, how was it that we thus appeared side by side in space? What was the real relation between us? But it would not do, I told myself, to continue these remote investigations, until I analysed much more carefully the nature of my own being as I am conscious of it in myself. No sooner had I thus brought my thoughts to a stand-still and compelled my interrogative energy to pause, while I pondered on the best path along which to begin this introspective self-analysis, than I was disturbed by observing that my companion, the being whom I had regarded, when I first awakened to consciousness, as part of myself, had left my side. Yes—though I daresay you, my dear Devil, have completely forgotten all this—you had leapt up from where we were lying together and bolted off. You moved as fast as the fastest meteorite I have ever been able, since those early days, to invent. I could soon perceive you far away in the distance, moving like the brightest of stars, towards some point on our horizon where you had seen, or where you imagined that you had seen, something that broke the hollow monotony of empty space.

"'So there are certainly two of us!' I said to myself, 'and I am not a double-being.'"

It was at this point in this curious dialogue above our heads between God and the Devil that the latter showed any interest in what the former was telling him. He had certainly wanted to hear the story, had been in fact extremely anxious to hear it; but it was clear to me, and I fancy to my Rhitha too, that the only thing he was really interested in was anything—it didn't matter what kind of thing—that concerned himself.

"Did you follow me with your eyes," the Devil now enquired of God, "until I had completely vanished over the horizon?"

"Yes," God replied, "I certainly did; but when you had disappeared I made no attempt to follow you, because I was absorbed in a discovery so astonishing to me and so fascinating to me that it occupied my attention to the exclusion of everything else."

At this point God became silent and so lost in thought that his companion grew obviously uneasy.

"What was that?" he asked.

But the Deity remained lost in thought. He may have been wondering how to put what he had to say in a manner that even his sensitive companion couldn't possibly find anything amusing in it; but what I, Gor of Blaenau-Ffestiniog, couldn't understand was the great difference between God as we saw him now, which was evidently what he really was and God as he had been shown to us in church and Sunday School. God as he really was turned out to be much more like myself in his thoughts and feelings than I ever could dream was possible! That God now, for instance, should be making such an effort to be solemn and serious in what he was telling the Devil, since he had seen that what disturbed the Devil most of all was any approach to humour, struck me as astonishingly natural and human. It was indeed not only human but humane, and certainly the opposite of what the Devil would have done. Meanwhile I, silly old Gor of Blaenau, as all my friends except Rhitha regarded me, now began to feel extremely proud of myself for my new discovery about the Cosmos, namely that one of its essential characteristics—whether derived from something jocular in its creator or from something in matter itself—is an element of humour. In other words, I told myself, the universe is a horribly comic spectacle, and it couldn't have been so if its creator hadn't had a definite liking for burlesque and farce, or if these things weren't already in the essence of matter itself.

"But you haven't yet told me," the Devil was now quite eagerly enquiring of God, "what you discovered in our surroundings in that desolate and empty vacuum that prevented you from following me in my rush to the horizon, where I am ready to confess now I fancied I saw, or really did see, something swimming or flying or floating or gliding."

"Well! I can tell you that at once, my dear Devil," said God. "What I discovered was that this Space into which you and I awoke was not as empty as I had first decided it was."

"You don't mean to say," cried the Devil, "that you saw other living things round us—things as living as we are, only clever at hiding themselves for fear we'd eat them up?"

"O no!" God replied, "I didn't see anything of that kind! What I saw was the fact that all round us the whole air was filled with floating fragments of solid substance. I whispered to these fragments of matter once or twice, and I deliberately touched some of them with certain antennæ or sensitized feelers that I willed to emerge from my person for that purpose; and what I found to be there was no more than a number of thick masses of formless substance, invisible at first glance, but easy to apprehend when once you came in contact with them. They did not fill the whole of the space round us, you must understand, but they floated there in larger or smaller fragments, and seemed to be swimming about there under the impulsion of the same sort of will or energy that you and I possessed, only how far resembling our consciousness I could not detect; for there was no response from any of these fragments of matter resembling my response to you or yours to me. I finally decided, after feeling about me as carefully and cautiously as I could, that these floating masses of substance possessed only rudimentary consciousness, that was still far below the level of the sort of power you and I possessed when we awoke in what at first I imagined to be entirely empty space, but in which you clearly thought you saw some living thing moving when you bolted off as you did to the furthest horizon of our vision."

"And so you decided—you are very fond of 'deciding,' aren't you, God?—that these fragments of substance floating about in space were quite different from you and me? They didn't have the five faculties of our five senses and their substance was neither animal nor vegetable. Am I right in thus describing your wonderful discovery, God?"

"Perfectly right, my dear Devil, perfectly right."

"And then, I take it," the Devil went on, "you decided—not a very striking decision, this time, you know—to play some game with these helpless lumps of matter? Am I right, my Lord?"

"You are certainly right. That indeed was exactly what I proposed to do."

"Did you think of asking these floating lumps whether they wanted to be played with?"

"I see what you are driving at, dear Devil! You would like me to confess that I derived pleasure from moulding these harmless blobs of matter into whatever fanciful shapes came into my head, and that if they didn't like such sport, this pleasure of mine was rather increased than diminished by their discomfort?"

"Well, isn't it? Only just a little tiny bit perhaps, but isn't it, just that little tiny bit?"

"No, my worthy Devil," God replied, "it isn't! Indeed, while we are upon this particular topic, I'd like to tell you this. Cast a glance down there, if you don't mind, on those four little creatures clinging to each other on that grassy fragment of the planet Earth, or Gaia, as the Greeks called her. You see that 'odd-one-out,' as you might call him who isn't fish, flesh, or fowl? Well, that creature was made in what its makers loved to call 'pure experiment', but declared sweetly that what they did was done for the sake of 'the little ones' of their race. The name they give to what they do is *vivisection*, a word that means cutting up into pieces what is still alive. They mustn't be confused with doctors, many of whom have been strongly opposed to such tortures. You could call them a set of men apart from all others, whose delight is in torturing what these earthlings call the 'lower animals' for the purpose of acquiring reactions. You, my dear Devil, were occupied in other things, in trying to make evil as much of an urge to destruction as I was—and still am—trying to make good an urge to creation; but I can assure you I had my eye on these wretches; and I think I made sure that the last moments of every one of them should resemble the last moments of the most miserable of the unfortunate animals they so enjoyed tormenting. But they are all gone now. Gone they are with the nebulæ and the galaxies, with the living stars and the dead stars, with the big stars and the little stars; gone they are with their planets and their satellites, gone to everlasting annihilation. I expect you have always imagined, my dear Devil, that I was deliberately lying to all my worshippers, whether Christian, Rabbinical, or Moslem, when I allowed them to believe in a life after death. No, my dear Devil, surprising as it may seem to you, I was *not* lying. The truth is, as I expect you could have discovered if you had given the matter any serious consideration, that in this whole matter of a life after death I am as ignorant as these quaint little earthlings are and as I think I may take for granted you are. I did not invent for them these worlds after death, of which their prophets and poets have made so much. I know no more about Heaven and Hell than they do, or than I fancy you do. In fact my own private suspicion is that there is no other world beyond this one, this rather empty one, in which we have now been left. Some of their philosophers have been talking lately about what they call 'another dimension'; but my own view of this 'other dimension' is simply that it is only another name for Annihilation, or sinking into Nothingness. But now, while we are discussing this matter of 'another dimension,' I want to confess to you a very important secret. Without the faintest idea that the world I created would ultimately of its own accord commit suicide, I have for many millenniums been pondering on the problem whether I couldn't create a world whose creatures would not be able to make one another as miserable as they have been able to do in the world that has just committed suicide. You know, my dear Devil, as well as I do, that it has been a mixture of Eastern and Western traditions, Jewish, Greek, Roman and African, that has led this world to the self-slaughter it has now consummated, and these traditions are all full of belief in other worlds, especially such worlds as Heaven and Hell. Well, old comrade, what I have been doing for thousands of years is trying to invent some very different kind of world, a world which it would be possible for me to create, but which would be quite different from the one that has just destroyed itself. I tell you this for the simple reason that I have no one else to whom I can tell it. Mind you, old friend, I shall not be at all disturbed if, on hearing of my tremendous scheme, you make up your mind at once to do all you can to render it futile, or even to destroy it root and branch. You and I have worked together so long in our contrarious fashion that, although we may each wish we could have our full fling independent of the other, my feeling is that we have the same idea at the back of our heads, namely that to get things moving with any sort of permanent success, it is essential that in the energy at work behind all that we do there must be both an element of creation and an element of destruction, or as those funny little creatures down there would put it, an element of good and an element of evil. Now, let us begin to describe my scheme, and do for the sake of empty space listen very carefully. In the first place let us make a world where every animal, whether human or subhuman, possesses a soul that can survive the death of its body. Next, let us see to it that this soul retains as much as is possible of its former personality, individuality, identity, and as much of its unique, peculiar, tastes, fancies, prejudices, humours, oddities, as can exist in a disembodied spirit."

What the Devil then asked was just what I, Gor Goginog of Blaenau, would certainly have asked, if I had had the gall to do so: "By your word *animal*, God, do you include all living creatures, such as birds and fish and reptiles and worms and insects—all that lives, in fact, save rocks and stones and trees and plants?"

God didn't hesitate for a second in his answer to this question; and I confess when I heard his answer, I pressed my Rhitha's hand with as much satisfaction as if I *had* asked this crucial question myself.

"Certainly I do. I include them all; every sort of living creature! I used the term 'animal' to make sure that you understood that I wasn't referring to lichens and toadstools and mushrooms. Perhaps what I ought to have emphasized more distinctly is the difference between forest-growths like funguses and such amphibious sea-shore growths as sea-anemones; but on this particular point I confess I feel rather dubious myself: but I certainly included all reptiles and all frogs and toads and newts and worms and every insect that exists. But leaving for a moment the rather ticklish question of creatures like sea-anemones, the scheme I am inclined to adopt for a completely New World suspended in Space is a scheme totally different from the one I adopted in the creation of the world that has now, of its own free will, disappeared forever! In one particular I intend to follow my former method of creating a world. Indeed, instead of changing, or even modifying it, I intend to pursue it to an even intenser extreme. I refer to my method in the creation of men and beasts and birds and fishes and reptiles and insects, of first envisaging in my own mind the sort of creatures I would like to see existing. Please understand that what I envisage in this way in my imagination is really like what you might think of as the soul of a creature before it has adapted itself to the surroundings in which it is destined to live; the sort of soul in fact that you can conceive, if you allow me, old friend, a little classical pedantry, to be waiting in limbo for its earthly incarnation. Now into this soul I shall pour all the energy possible for a self-creating exploration of matter. And I shall do this with every creature I create.

"No! Don't interrupt me just yet, old friend, till I've told you more about my New World. You know what we do ourselves, my dear Devil, in regard, I mean, to our own appearance? We appear of course completely different to every conscious being who confronts us. But the interesting thing is that, while in ourselves we are so vividly aware of being able to take any shape we please, we ourselves have persuaded ourselves quite naturally and spontaneously to think of ourselves with human bodies—that is to say with bodies resembling those of Adam, the first man. Between ourselves we can entirely discard the account of the Beginning of things which I dictated to the scribes of Israel; whereby you, the destroyer, are represented as a leering serpent, and I, the creator, as an austere and forbidding old gentleman, carried through Space by a crowd of mischievous boys and provocative angels! I selected the Children of Israel as the recipients of the revelation of my identity in the matter of Adam and Eve, because I have always had a special fondness for Jews. It was this partiality that led me to select Jesus of Nazareth as the one descendant of Adam whose inmost soul and instinctive gestures seemed almost akin to my own. What always made me angry seemed always to make him angry, and what always made me want to cry seemed always to make him want to cry. I have often committed impulsive and foolish mistakes in my quick moods, both for good and for harm; and so did he! The longer he lived the more deeply he came to resemble me, so that he was perfectly justified in his daring idea that we were father and son. Through all the æons of years that you and I have lived together, since the day we found ourselves side by side in empty space, the worst twinge of sorrow and remorse I have ever felt was when I heard those heart-rending words: 'Eloi! Eloi! Lama Sabachthani!'

"But now listen very seriously to my words. As you have

seen, and no doubt your own influence with its instinct for destruction had a lot to do with it, the world I created, as my worshippers love to put it 'in the Beginning,' has been brought to an end by the loathing of life felt by the galaxies, nebulæ, stars, planets and satellites, together with all the creatures, human and otherwise, not excepting all the worms, insects, reptiles and saurians, that filled the whole expanse of the earth, with all her forests, all her grassy slopes, all her rocky ridges and stony peaks, all her reedy swamps and her pebbly and sandy sea-shores, yes! and with all her memories too, memories going back to the days when I tried in vain to make Adam, the first man, and Eve, the first woman, do what was wise, and what I wanted them to do, and avoid doing what would bring disaster. Very good. All that is over now! I created the world. It lasted for several millions of years. Then, because of the miseries and sufferings which men and women inflicted upon one another, and because of the horrors that went on, in every direction, as much among the tiny insects as among wild beasts and savage birds, the whole creation, whether pushed on to it by you or not, committed a universal suicide, leaving us and those quaint little objects down there alone together in empty space.

"I don't think either of us two, neither you, who know me far better, I fully allow, than any of my worshippers, nor I, who know you better than any of *your* worshippers, fully realize the condition of those pitifully rent and torn souls who worship me, and who struggle so madly to kill half of their natures in the illusion, instigated by their priests and pastors, that I have forbidden all sexual satisfaction—these poor wretches who are called saints—or of the unhappy, brooding, desperate, dark, mad, lonely, lurid stirrers of weird cauldrons, into which they throw appalling substances, who worship you, and are called 'black magicians,' or how we ought to have made it clear to them both that it is only out of the clash between you and me, and out of the perpetual struggle between you and me, that life can go on at all! With me alone as the ruler all would stagnate; and with you alone as the ruler all would disappear!

"Well now, consider this point, Devil my dear, and consider it very, very carefully. You will remember how I decided to give to every creature I created—from Leviathan and Behemoth to the smallest water-rat and star-fish, from Adam and Eve and Cain and Abel to the tiniest bee that buzzed through their flower-beds and to the smallest monkey that swung from branch to branch above their heads; yes! from the noblest ox in their pastures to the daintiest little lamb in their well-guarded sheepfolds—the unique gift, however they misused it, of free will? You always predicted—and you were, as we now have seen by this universal cosmic suicide, perfectly right in predicting—that this gift of free will to such crazy creatures would end in disaster. But it seemed to me that a world without free will, a world ruled by absolute determinism from the start, would be so dull and tedious an experiment as to be hardly worth making.

"But now, confronted by this cosmogonic self-destruction, evidently due to the fact that, endowed with free will, all the living things in earth, air and water, by devouring each other, by meddling with each other, by making each other's existence intolerable, turned the world into such a hell that the only way out of it was universal suicide, it has entered my head, though I daresay there exist insuperable objections which will present themselves later, that it would be of great interest to create an absolutely predetermined universe of living beings not one among whom possessed the faintest semblance of free-will. I am thinking of a universe in which every house-fly, every daddy-long-legs, every beetle, every butterfly, every moth, along with all the toads and frogs and newts and tadpoles, and along with all the reptiles, and along with all the birds of the air and the fish of the sea and the wild beasts of the jungle and the men, women, and children of country and town, are all driven by an absolutely inescapable law of inflexible determinism, much more implacable than the Greek Moira or even than that still more unbendable and rigidly physical pressure that Homer was wont to call 'Anangke.'

"Now, can't you imagine, my dear Devil, that having worked out this undeviating cause-and-effect universe, in which all its children, human and otherwise, have no choice at all, and know they have no choice, but just drift on and on, like predestined ripples in a calm sea, and supposing I had the power to make every single creature that lived, while it lived, extremely joyous and happy—can't you imagine, I say, speaking in the terms of those earthlings below us down there, that such a universe could be a far more desirable one for its occupants than the one that has recently disappeared?"

"Why the hell don't you ask them then, you old blunderbuss of a Nursery-God playing with picture-blocks of wood? Call them up here and ask them! I'll be mightily tickled to hear what they say! Each of them, of *that*, I can assure you already, will say something different!"

I, Gor Goginog of Blaenau, having heard this, was, as you may believe, not a little startled. But I thought to myself, there's no reason to draw back in fear. The Devil can't hurt us with God there, and God won't send us to hell if the Devil doesn't want us! And as I looked at Org's antediluvian and amphibious left eye, though it bulged a good deal more out of his head than was usual, I could see that he too had grasped the proposition and was favourable to it. The girls seemed less certain in their minds; but with one of my usual rapid flights of mythological imagination, I put this down entirely to the absence, up there, above our heads, in that enormous, aerial, chilly space, of any feminine hostess! What was wanting I told myself was simply the presence of the Virgin Mary. The presence of Her Son would have disturbed me and disturbed Org, too, well did I know *that*! Yes, "the Mother of God" was what we wanted, since we were going to Heaven, and not to Olympus!

However, there was a feminine being behind all of us, or to speak more correctly, *under* all of us, who was quite ready and determined to be our Earthly Mother at this important interview. I refer of course to the grassy plain on which we were standing and which had brought us here through so many extraordinary shocks; yes! and not only through the vanishing away of Time, but of Eternity too.

And now this heroic fragment of Gaia, the ancient earth, was actually carrying us up where we might talk with God.

What I found particularly interesting, after our grassy landscape had settled itself down and we were really in what I think I have a perfect right to call Heaven, were the forms our two entertainers assumed as they talked to us there. For without a moment's delay they both joined our little party of four on our floating field of grass. God had the form of an old gentleman with a long curly beard and rough curly hair. He was evidently quite naked under his garments which consisted of heavy robes one above another and by no means very elegantly arranged; and his ankles and feet were quite bare. In fact he exactly resembled the Eternal Being in the picture of Adam and Eve by Arazzo Fiammingo in the Galleria Accademia in Florence. The Devil's appearance, as he squatted on the grass between Org and Asm on one side and Rhitha and me on the other, was even easier to describe, for he was the very image of the particular one of the demonic chimeras on the top of Notre Dame looking down on Paris, who is described in the guide books as "The Thinker" and who has a short horn in the centre of his head, a couple of folded wings about his shoulders, and a dangerous-looking tongue protruding from his mouth.

It took no time at all for us four earthlings to get the spirit of the occasion; and I thought, "I suppose this is a supreme example of the kind of thing that happens over and over again in life, when some miraculously unexpected concatenation of events whirls us into a situation about which we have told ourselves exciting stories since infancy. Here we actually were in empty space alone with God and the Devil and invited by them to give advice as to the creation of a fresh world."

It was in fact God who spoke first.

"We have," he began, "or more accurately with the help of my good friend the Devil, I have been planning a world as absolutely opposite to the one that has just committed suicide as can be imagined. In the first place I have decided that there shall be *no* free will. No free decisions at all. By that I mean that every man, woman and child, every beast and bird, every worm and insect shall just give itself up to the affairs of its life, one after another, as custom and habit, instinct and natural desire move it and draw it on, without having to decide anything. It will feel itself to be a conscious unit, a conscious dot, a conscious grain, a conscious pebble, a conscious seed, and will enjoy the sensation of being forced along by fate and necessity without having to decide one single thing for itself. It won't be able to pause or stop for a second in the stream of cause and effect, but it will be prepared quite happily and resignedly for its death when its hour shall come. I have been thinking—and this is a point upon which I should be very glad to ask the advice of each one of you four beings—about eliminating from this fresh world, in which every creature will resemble a joyous sunlit ripple in an irresistible tide, certain ravenous, venomous, and voracious creatures that feed upon others, such as lions and tigers, eagles, hawks, kites, crows, vultures and poisonous serpents, together with sharks, sword-fish, and other ferocious and predatory inhabitants of the ocean. It has occurred to me that it might be a good thing to put an end, once and for all, to the unpleasant habit, whether in earth, air, or water, of creatures eating each other and living upon each other. Why not have a world in which men and beasts and birds and fishes and reptiles and worms and saurians and insects feed, not on each other, but purely and entirely on *vegetation*? Thus all sea-creatures would feed on weeds of the sea and all land creatures on the vegetable growths of fields and forests, of swamps and fens.

"But here, my dear young earthlings—I use the word 'young' because from your terrestrial calculation both I, and my old associate the Devil, are fantastically and fabulously old—and I want to ask you four persons, personally and individually, a significant question. Quite apart from their particular place in the general scheme of things, are there any special creatures that you four, or one of you four, would be thankful to have excluded from the living inhabitants of our fresh world?"

We all looked at each other and there was a momentary hesitation. Then to my surprise, and also I confess a little to my disappointment, for I would have preferred that my little Rhitha should have looked with wonder at me, her man, having the boldness and courage and cleverness to speak, instead of speaking herself, my girl fearlessly cried: "Couldn't *fleas* be left out of the fresh World?"

God glanced hurriedly at the Devil who gave a significant nod, as much as to say, "I'll be on tap to supply *that* deficiency with a few well-aimed pricks of conscience!" And thus reassured, God conceded the point. "Yes, we will eliminate fleas."

I was very anxious to think of some creature the choice of which for elimination would impress both God and the Devil, and also display a strikingly wide biological knowledge of Nature as well as a pathological understanding of human aversions. But Org's girl Asm spoke up before I had decided upon the creature whose absence from life for the next couple of thousand years would be the greatest blessing to us mortals.

"O please!" cried Asm eagerly.

"Speak up, child," said God kindly.

"Let's have no bed-bugs!"

God actually gave a deep-throated chuckle at this, and the Devil made a vicious scoop with his tongue as if snatching up one of the insects in question.

"Yes, my child," agreed the Creator, "not a single bed-bug shall enter our world, not from the north, or the south, or the east, or the west, not from zenith to nadir, shall a single bed-bug slip in. Isn't that so?" And God glanced not without a shade of anxiety it seemed to me, at his diabolic partner.

"Not a single one," agreed that enemy of all life; and it struck me, as he uttered this final doom for all bed-bugs that the antagonist of creation looked more like one of those chimera-demons gazing down on Paris from the summit of Notre Dame, as he wagged his worm-like tongue from side to side between his hollow lips and drew his muscular wings nearer to the solitary horn on the top of his head, than he had ever done before. Indeed he looked as if he intended to visit every bedroom in Paris that night as a snapper-up of bed-bugs.

It was at this point, while I was swallowing my humiliation at not having thought of any desirable omission from our newly created world, which apparently was to resemble a deterministic earthly paradise continued forever, that Org lifted up his multi-genetic voice, a voice that suggested paws, feathers, tails. And do you know what Org wanted eliminated? Nothing less than *lice*!

"Yes indeed, my friend," responded God in the most indulgent tone he had yet used. "Do you agree, my dear Devil?" And the snort that emerged from some portion of the Devil's person, was a sufficient answer. There were to be no more lice.

It was at this point that my special kind of egoism—whether a natural mixture of pride, vanity, and conceit or some form of wild and reckless impulse I cannot say, but whatever it was had been a peculiarity of mine all my life and it had been intensified since I fell in love with Rhitha—asserted itself to a degree I found it impossible to restrain.

"I have lately been impressed," I began, in my most rhetorical, oratorical, and leading actor's tone, "by constant references to the existence of *another dimension* beyond this one in which we now abide as we stand together on this beautiful green plain, which is so like the fens of Norfolk, with a misty horizon surrounding us on all sides.

"The dimension in which we now exist, as we stand here, clearly makes only one demand for its cosmic environment, namely Space. There was an epoch when it made another, namely Time, but that epoch is at an end; for Time has been destroyed. Now as thou, O God, and as thou also, O Devil, know well, the chief value of the dimension in which we now all live is its adaptability to the existence of, and to the necessity for, our bodies, and our bodily feelings and our bodily movements. But, Thou O mighty God, and Thou also, O mighty Devil, know very well that it is possible for all living creatures, from whales and hippopotamuses to newts and tadpoles, from giants like Samson or Goliath to the smallest of pygmies, to lose themselves in their thoughts till they completely forget their bodies and are indeed quite literally 'out of their bodies.' Well! This is our present situation. Here we all are on this brave scrap of our old Mother Earth that has heroically refused to follow the rest of the astronomical world and commit suicide; and now I am quite sure that although she is only a portion of her mother, of our planetary mother, Gaia, the ancient Earth, she has inherited, just as the rest of us have inherited, a conscious mind as well as a sensitive body. Now you may be sure that this conscious mind, independently of the body to which it is attached, can lose itself in its thoughts and forget its body altogether just as we can forget ours. This being so, O most mighty God, this being so, O most mighty Devil, I propose that, with the help of the mind of the earth beneath our feet, we boldly make a desperate leap, and turn our minds away from our bodies altogether and forget our bodies altogether and with one terrific act of faith leap into this other dimension. If we make this desperate leap into this other dimension, we *shall* reach it, and we shall find ourselves all together in a world composed of nothing but conscious minds, minds that need no bodies, feel no bodies, see no bodies, minds that are simply and purely minds and apprehend one another's thoughts by direct contact of thought with thought!"

I became silent and looked around. I looked at Rhitha. I looked at Asm. I looked at Org. I looked at the Devil. I looked at God. I confess I was absolutely beside myself with satisfaction at having made this speech. If you asked me what it was that inspired me to utter it, I would be unable to reply. It came into my head; and it had to come out in the way it did.

I was certainly extremely surprised, and I have an inkling that we all were, when the answer to my oration came, after quite a pause, from God Himself.

"Yes, I have heard of this 'other dimension,' and so I think have you, my dear Devil." As God spoke, he glanced quickly at his companion; who, I noticed, gave a faint shake to his head, and a faint shrug to his shoulders. "But I am not ashamed," God went on, "to confess to you four, or to you, O noblest of fragments, whose mind, I shrewdly suspect to be behind this thought which has come into the head of Gor Goginog of Blaenau, that I have for thousands of years wondered whether such a leap as you describe from our world of objective space, in which heads and arms and bodies and legs and eyes and ears and noses and mouths correspond with the air we breathe and the aerial unendingness that surrounds us—whether, I say, such a leap as you describe, full of a desperate faith, might not lead to surprising results.

"Some of the New Testament *logoi*, those mystically-pious oracles of the Jews who followed Jesus, announce that we have faith, hope, and love left to help us, and that of these three the most effective is love. This is a great mistake. Hope and love are comforting and reassuring, and make the life both of Gods and men, calmer, pleasanter, happier: but neither hope nor love can work miracles. Faith alone can do that. If you ask me *why*, my answer is simple. Because while love unites us with the object of the miracle, and while hope keeps us alive while the object of the miracle is being approached; it is faith and faith alone that works it. So when you talk of this leap into this mysterious other dimension, to which we both have been hearing obscure references for some time, I am ready to risk it, and I believe my old partner and confederate-antagonist here is also willing to risk it. But you must realize, my little ones, that this is a very serious risk for me; for I have just been planning a fresh world on wholly and completely different lines from our old one that has now committed suicide. In this fresh world which I have been planning, not only will there be, as you earthlings have suggested, no fleas, no bed-bugs, and no lice, no vultures, no sharks, no boa-constrictors, but all will be *pre-determined*, and there will be no free will leading to wickedness and cruelty and disaster. I just tell you this, my dears, and my old antagonist here agrees for once with what I say, in order to prove that whatever risks you four may be taking in this plunge, I shall be taking a lot more! You will be risking your four lives; but I shall be risking my new fresh world, created *free from free will* and likely to bring into being millions upon millions of happy lives. You must remember that this soul of the fragment of your old earth that has put this leap into your heads though it risks more than your lives, doesn't, like I do, risk a whole new universe. You may well ask me why I consent to take this leap. I will tell you why. I take it out of pure weariness. You think, because I am God, I am tireless. Not at all! At this particular epoch I feel more tired than you can possibly believe. In fact I feel tired out. And you also must remember that those preposterous opposites—that were no real opposites at all, but just a pair of ghoulish phantasms invented by a set of tricky mathematicians and a set of still more tricky theologians, and called by them Time and Eternity—are now gone for good. Neither time nor eternity have ever had any reality outside the schools and the churches and the governments. Nothing delights any authority more than the splitting up of Time into various-shaped little pieces of goblinish excrement, and then marshalling these lively if not very odoriferous turdlings into 'round games' of various sorts! As for Eternity, *that*, of course, has always been only another name for the precipitation into a foul and fetid cloud of that special smell of choir-stall cushions and communion-rail mats, which has come to be associated with spiritual awe and solemn silence. In reality, as a great many young people would at once, if they only dared to speak out, freely confess, this holy silence in the presence of all the altars in the world rouses them to simple revolt. By yielding to this holy silence and by being scared by this holy silence, your healthy-minded youth, both male and female, all over the earth give up their right of being themselves in favour of the cunning craftiness of the sly and selfish rascals who are playing their old historic games. When I think of all the crimes committed in my name with such subtlety, I feel ready, I tell you, to jump into any other dimension, if only I could end my nauseating weariness of the whole business of creation. It has become, I tell you, intolerable to me to think of how your earthlings have come to associate my name with that particularly unpleasant, malodorous *hush* before my altar at the heart of which is really, I am quite sure, simply a natural human horror of charnel-houses, corpses, and vampirish ghosts.

"No, I have not missed, any more than has my old friend the Devil, these recent hints among your sages about 'another dimension.' But I confess, as indeed is natural, considering my concern over what has happened to the universe I created, and my longing to create one not only free from bugs and fleas and lice but totally different from the one that has now gone, that I shall be risking more than any of you little ones if I do take this leap. I swear to you I have spent more energy than any other creator-god has ever spent over his work! But I admit that by endowing the creatures of my creation with free will, I did risk what has now happened, namely their almost universal decision to bring the whole thing to an end. In this fresh World I have been lately devising our creatures would be unable to do this. Driven forward by an inescapable chain of cause-and-effect, they would just drift along like ripples in a calm sea or like waves in a rough sea. All will be determined: all will be inevitable: all will be fate: and all the creatures in our new world, including whatever solar systems and zodiacal constellations we may choose to create in place of those that have rushed to destruction, will have to find themselves accepting without question the necessity for just going on as we newly and freshly fashion them, without deciding one single thing for themselves. They will have to take for granted that as we have fashioned them, so it will always be. I am perfectly aware that, as there is much to be said in favour of this deterministic world, so there is also much to be said against it. Now if we two, companions in super-consciousness, and you four, companions in normal consciousness, are all of us really prepared to take the risk of this leap or plunge, or whatever you like to call it, into this 'other dimension,' which may or may not exist at all, we must keep well in mind what we are risking. We are risking extinction. What we've got to remember, my dear Devil," God went on, "is that you and I are at bottom just as ignorant of the ultimate reality of things as are these pathetic little human creatures, whose imagination in its longing for an all-powerful creator would have invented me, and in its dread of an all-powerful destroyer would have invented you, if we hadn't already, neither of us knows how, found ourselves alive in an empty space. This new idea which has just come into the heads of these mathematical metaphysicians, about another dimension, has been an old worry to me. For millions upon millions of years it has been darting in and out of my mind, and I am sure I must have murmured to you something, once in a few thousand years, about such a thing. But of course you've always been so busy trying to bring to nothing my various schemes for easing the general situation that you probably hardly listened to this other matter.

"What I have been wondering of late, if I can have your attention for a moment now, is whether you and I haven't been too sure of our own immunity from annihilation. We have watched these Greek deities hover over the heads of their dying favourites and then rush back to Father Zeus the moment they themselves are hurt; and we've watched those Indian sages, like the Buddha, leave their peaceful Nirvana and go back to their peaceful Nirvana, as their mood has varied between a longing for action and a longing for inaction. And now we have seen the human race commit suicide, and the stars commit suicide, and all the conscious creatures in this world I created and to which I gave free will make up their minds to join this universal self-slaughter, so as to escape once for all the miseries and sufferings of life.

"Now I must confess to you, my dear Devil, that I have been thinking for some while of creating a world on totally different lines from the one which has destroyed or is in the act of destroying itself. This fresh world of mine, as I have already tried to explain to you, will be completely ruled by the rigid determination of cause-and-effect. It will be a world without the faintest spark of free will. But the more I think of such a world the more it strikes me as hopelessly flat and dull. Free will *may* have led to suicide; but neither it, nor the suicide it has led to, could be called flat or dull. So between—I mustn't say between 'the devil and the deep sea'—but between this dull determination and this deadly free will I am at my wits' end. And what I am now tempted to suggest is that you and I imitate these creatures I created, and throw over the whole tiresome business, *and commit suicide ourselves*! I have decided you know, my dear old enemy, that this 'other dimension' they talk about is simply another name for everlasting death. So why, in the name of eternal escape, shouldn't *we* try it? Now I expect you four creatures from the planet where Adam and Eve lived in their earthly paradise in complete innocence are finding it rather hard to believe that I, God, the creator of that paradise and of the human pair who lived in it, am taking the same risk as you four take when we make this leap into this other dimension. But I *am* taking this risk, and so is my ancient companion, the Devil, who was born side by side with me in this same endless, limitless empty Space, in which we, six conscious existences, find ourselves today. In the long reverential years, thousands upon thousands of them, of the worship with which the human race has worshipped us, the majesty and glory and power with which I have been endowed, have increased to a point, I suppose it has been the same with all gods worshipped by humanity, the same with the good old Kronos, the father of Zeus, as with the East Indian Brahma, to a point at which we get the title of 'The Absolute' given us by philosophers, very much as your politicians of today reward a plain mister by turning him into a marquis.

"I have had, as you mortals would put it, 'very funny feelings,' when I have tried to imagine myself this blessed 'Absolute.' As far as I have been able to follow your theologians, the 'Absolute' is just simply *everything that exists*; so that not only all the scum in the world and all the dirt in the world and all the bugs and fleas and lice and maggots and worms in the world, but all the un-vomited vomit and all the undissipated phlegm and all the dung that hasn't yet been ejected by our bowels are essential portions of my *absolute person*. Now when I consider myself in this way I feel decidedly queer: indeed, to tell you the exact truth, I feel not a little nauseated. Well? Are we all ready? And don't forget, my dear four, and don't *you* forget either, my dear Devil, that among us six conscious beings who are risking extinction by this leap into another dimension, I am the one who am risking the most, because I am the one who am a million times fuller than you are of that particular kind of energy that your philosophers love to describe as the Life-Force. You see what we are really going to do is not merely to leap, as we might say 'out of our skins,' but *out of our minds* too. In fact we are going to leap out of everything that we know at present as ourselves and as what is not ourselves, and as above or under or around ourselves; in fact we are going to leap out of the whole system of ourselves and other selves, and out of the whole system of earth, air, water and fire, of suns, moons, planets and stars, out of the whole world that hitherto has meant to us all that we call life. Well? Are you all ready? Off we go!"

It can be imagined how tightly I clutched the fingers of my precious Rhitha as we made our leap; and I fancy our queer monster Org did the same, if his powers of adhesion could be so described, with his lovely girl Asm.

Well, it was done! And the queer thing was that I found I was not in the faintest degree surprised by the result. The result was in fact just what I had expected. This is surely very odd? It is so odd that if anybody else had told *me* as, "out of the blue," shall we say, or through the magnetized voice of one of those queer people we call "mediums," I am now telling *you*, I would regard it as so impossible that I should boldly say that "the spirit," or whatever it was that talked to the "medium", was simply telling lies! How *could* I possibly have expected it? In the first place it was entirely different from, in fact it was directly opposite to, every single thing that God had just been predicting. I can only think that a person who is just stupidly conceited in the simple way that I am is so ordinary and so completely like everybody else that, in his lack of intellect and imagination, he has never in any true sense taken in this world so that any "dimension" would, to his thick-skinned imperviousness, be no different from another "dimension." An even more natural and inevitable cause of my complete lack of surprise at the nature of this "other dimension," when we dived into it, was the fact that my nature is so animal—and I warrant our friend Org felt just the same in this—that my first instinctive recoil from any expected shock is to sink back into a sort of pre-natal trance, half drowsy lethargy and half a deliberate indrawing of an observant turtle-like head into a protective shell.

Let me indeed go so far as to say that every being who possesses a body, when threatened with that body's death, tends to become all in a moment curiously interested in what it is losing. And here I could bring forward an argument that really does seem to refute the prognostications of God. I refer to the fact that in the crucial moment before making our plunge and diving into "the deep end" of this confounded "other dimension," we all began considering our bodies very, *very* carefully. God considered his bare feet and his long curly beard. The Devil considered the dry leathery movements of his tongue between his fibrous lips. And we all did the same. Both girls lifted their free hands to the back of their heads to arrange their hair. I gazed at my knees praying that they wouldn't show outwardly the shakiness they felt inwardly; and old Org scratched the least seemly part of his huge frame. And how eminently characteristic it was of the rhetorical but essentially commonplace orator that I am, that the first words I uttered were the most commonplace of all human descriptions of death.

"Well!" I said. "We have joined the Majority!"

My next thought, if thought it can be called, was an extremely simple and natural one. I wanted to be sure that Rhitha was close to me, although neither of us possessed here, it seemed, any hands to hold! But no sooner had I thought of her than our thoughts were together, for she too had thought of me. My "we are together still" corresponded with her, "we are still together"; and we each felt the other's personality give a sigh of infinite relief. It was together, therefore, that we both soon realized that Org and our exquisite Asm were also close to us. But where was God and the Devil?

We had all discovered by this time that it was possible in this universal sea of death to follow every single thought that our companions had. "And what," I wondered, "would be the best word in our old earth-language for the queer over-lapping of consciousness that apparently goes on in Death's great ocean?"

I resolved to make an effort to find out.

"What word shall I use," I asked God, "for the way we exchange our consciousness of things down here?"

I had no sooner asked this question than I realized I was rudely interrupting a very interesting conversation that was going on between Him and the Devil.

"What would you say, Devil, my dear, to this young fellow's question?"

I didn't at all like being called "a young fellow." Indeed I felt that this whole leap of ours into this strange sea was not due either to God or the Devil, but was entirely due to me and to my interest in modern philosophy and my acquaintance with the whole metaphysical notion of *different dimensions*. But I suppressed my peevishness as well as I could, so as not to miss anything in the Devil's answer to God's question.

"Tell the silly kid," replied the Devil, "what I've just been told by a friend of mine down here called Moloch, whom the Olympian God has killed with a thunderbolt, that in this dimension answers to questions come from the *tone* in which they are asked and not from any reply! But *who hears the tone*? Can the person who asks hear his own 'tone'? Such was the question," continued the Devil, "that I asked my friend Moloch and he said——"

But I could endure no longer at this crisis to listen to Moloch's ramblings.

"Please, please God!" I interrupted: "tell me, I pray and beseech you, what is the difference between this 'dimension' and the ordinary 'next world' to which we all go when we die?"

"Shall I tell him?" God enquired of the Devil.

"What do I care?" answered this latter.

"You consider then, Devil, old friend," said God, "that since we're all in the same sea, it doesn't matter what we tell each other?"

"Not a damn," replied the Devil.

"Well, I'll be frank with you four," said God quietly, "since we took the plunge together. The truth is I never for a moment dreamed that this place, which your metaphysicians call another dimension, would turn out to be nothing less than the old familiar 'next world,' a world that my friend the Devil here and I have known to exist all our lives, though being what we are, we have only seen people descend into it without being able or without wishing to follow them. But now that we *have* followed them: it seems to me that as far as that great, empty, endless Space, hitherto the House of the Living, is concerned, the Devil and I are in the 'next world' with the rest. I even catch myself feeling—which is more than *you* do, friend Devil, isn't it?—a curious pitiful tenderness for this same vast endless, limitless, empty Space, that we two, along with you four, have deserted. I almost feel as if *it* were, or as if *she* were, the vast forsaken grandmother of all that has ever lived. Don't *you* feel a little like that too, O heroic spirit, thou soul of that deserted green patch of earth which was part of the body of the planet Earth?"

While God's voice was dying away, I, Gor Goginog of Blaenau, became aware of two amazing things. The first of these was that the green landscape, from which we had jumped when we jumped out of our bodies, had vanished with our bodies. The second was that a powerful, beautiful, and extremely sensitive mind that made me think of Persephone herself, when she was carried off by Pluto as she gathered flowers, was now actually in touch with us, and that she was assuring me that the same spirit which had made her refuse to commit suicide now made her fully, entirely, utterly, and thankfully resign herself to annihilation and extinction. Although my senses were gone with my body and I could see nothing, I had the feeling that, if I only *could* see the utterer of these tremendous thoughts, the figure I should see would be beautiful with the quite special and peculiar beauty of a figure upon an Etruscan vase, and I began to feel an incredible comfort in being saved from the fear of death. And then a curious thing happened, if it is possible to use the word "happened" for such an event, namely a lapse in the usual perfect reciprocity between myself and Rhitha.

"What a relief," I thought, taking for granted that Rhitha would, as she generally has done, wholly agree with everything that came into my head, a head which I felt to be much more capable of intellectual thoughts than her lovely little noddle, "to be already dead without knowing it! And how wonderful it is to think that it was at my suggestion and nobody else's though God did at once, I admit, agree with the idea, that we all so boldly plunged into this curious place! There can be no limit, my dear, can there, to this great death-ocean, since it has to contain all the souls of all the beings begotten by all worlds that have ever existed, together with the souls of those worlds themselves, for worlds must have souls, if their offspring have them, mustn't they? And shall I now, my lovely one, with equal boldness—for I *am* a bold one, aren't I, my pet? —ask God whether there's any reality down here corresponding to Hell, Purgatory, and Paradise, or to those older places such as Acheron, Tartarus, Erebus, and Styx?"

I had no sooner communicated this thought of mine to Rhitha than I became aware that she was hardly following me. Her thoughts, it was clear to me, were elsewhere; and this, I confess, made me feel indignant. And as a result of my indignation I addressed my thoughts to our old monster Org.

"Shall we explore a little?" I asked him. "Wouldn't it be exciting if we could meet down here some of those old Biblical characters we were always hearing about? No! I don't mean St. Paul! He'd hang on to us and talk of nothing but Pharisees and Caesars and Roman citizens and thorns in the flesh and what he heard on the road to Damascus; and he'd want to know whether we came from Libya or Pamphylia or had once had friends in Caesar's household. No! I mean those wonderful old Jews like Moses and Noah and Samson and Solomon and Joshua the son of Nun, and women like Sarah and Rachel and Rebecca and Jael the wife of Heber the Kenite! Oh yes! Org, old friend, shall you and I ask God or the Devil if we can't have a word with Achilles and Ajax the son of Telamon, and that sweet war-man Hector, and even with Argive Helen herself! And just think how wonderful it would be to talk with Richard Coeur-de-Lion and to ask Rabelais about his hospital and about his printing-shop and about his visit to Rome!"

But I received no reply of any sort from Org; and this silence of the only other earthborn male in our little group brought my spirits down with a considerable collapse. And then it came over me that Rhitha's consciousness was communicating something very important to my consciousness; and I fancy, if it had been necessary to utter those quaint noises we were accustomed to call words in order to convey her meaning, what she would have said was something like this: "Darling Gor, please don't be slow in taking in the fact that the whole thing's over. God and the Devil are both dead. Didn't you hear a voice cry, 'It is finished,' and another voice murmur in response: '*Abyssus invocat abyssum*'?"

So it had happened! God and the Devil were already dead; and in any second now both Rhitha and I would be dead. Shall I have time to compose before I go some really wonderful "last words"?

But who will hear my "last words"? Oh, I do so, so, so want somebody, somewhere, to hear them! I want somebody, somewhere, to know how deeply I understood the best Greek and Latin poets! Yes! It's to *you*, somebody, somewhere, that I'm talking now! All my life I've only wanted two things—to enjoy myself, whatever's happening, and to lecture somebody else on how he or she can enjoy whatever's happening! I want to perform, to act, to play the clown, to show off as a philosopher; and how can I enjoy all this when I am nothing and there's nobody there! There *must* be somebody there, there must, there must, there must, there *must* be somebody! Well, you, whoever you are and wherever you are, are that somebody! Rhitha was the one person I wanted to live with. I could live without Org and Asm! I could live without God. But I couldn't live without Rhitha. And so, now that we're both dying, I *must* have you, whoever you are, to hear my last words!

Whether my Rhitha and her lovely friend Asm are being long enough in their dying to exchange that mysterious young girl's smile, which only da Vinci of all men who have ever lived seemed able to catch before it vanished, I do not know: and if it *did* pass between them, I shall never know whether my barbaric naivety had helped to evoke it; but this I *do* know, that from my mouth out of the throat of that ultimate Void which in Welsh we call "Diddym," and that had already swallowed up God and the Devil, there rose into the air the recklessly defiant Homeric words: *alla kai empes*—"all the same for that," immediately followed by the famous summing up of Catullus:

> *Soles occidere et redire possunt*
> *Nobis cum semel occidit brevis lux*
> *Nox est perpetua una dormienda.*

> "Suns are able to rise and set
> But for us when once our brief day is done
> There is only a night of perpetual sleep."

www.ingramcontent.com/pod-product-compliance
Lightning Source LLC
Chambersburg PA
CBHW030611310726
48979CB00003B/665

* 9 7 8 0 6 4 8 9 2 0 4 3 4 *